# Praise for *The Laughter of Strangers*

"Like a ghost fretting over its lost body (or is it bodies? – in this book whatever you think of as 'you' might simply float like a butterfly right into someone else's body) a boxer attests to his presence, damaged and shimmery though it may be. That this fractured first person narrator feels the need to put the word 'me' in quotes speaks volumes. Terrifying volumes. This elastic, hurtling narrative pivots (and pivots again) on a recurring image of almost unimaginable dread – that of being laughed at in your hour of need by an audience of strangers."

—**GRACE KRILANOVICH**, author of *The Orange Eats Creeps*

"The last time I got punched in the face (by someone I wasn't married to or dating) I was 16 years old. What began as an exchange of witty banter, turned into a pummeling. Never make jokes about a man's mother enjoying the erotic companionship of goats, or you'll find out about this world. *The Laughter of Strangers* is like that beating. I never trust people who use a middle initial, but Michael J Seidlinger is different. If *The Laughter of Strangers* had a middle initial it would be an F. And that F would stand for "Fuck yes." I'm on my back. I'm having my behavior corrected. It's teaching me a lesson. And I can see stars."

—**SCOTT MCCLANAHAN**, author of *Crapalachia*

"Michael J. Seidlinger's *The Laughter of Strangers* is vicious and unforgettable. Willem Floures's search for meaning in a world that keeps knocking him off his feet is as gritty and enthralling as a fight. The Laughter of Strangers destroyed my expectations of what a boxing novel can be. Seidlinger is charting new narrative territory, and we should follow him wherever he goes."

—**LAURA VAN DEN BERG**, author of *The Isle of Youth*

"Steeped in noir, Michael J Seidlinger's superb boxing novel delivers 12 rounds of sweet science and shifting identities. Both physical and philosophical, it'll leave the reader with a complicated bruise – the closer you examine it, the more it resembles your own face."

—**JEFF JACKSON**, author of *Mira Corpora*

# The Laughter of Strangers

## by Michael J Seidlinger

A Lazy Fascist Novel

Lazy Fascist Press
an imprint of Eraserhead Press
205 NE Bryant Street
Portland, Oregon 97211

www.lazyfascistpress.com

ISBN: 978-1-6210-5097-1

Edited by Cameron Pierce

Proofread by Andrew Wayne Adams and Kirsten Alene

Printed in the USA.

# WILLEM FLOURES

| Sex | Male |
|---|---|
| Manager/Trainer | Spencer Mullen |
| Division | Heavyweight |
| Rating | 1 / 57 |
| Stance | Southpaw |
| Height | 6'1" |
| Reach | 70" |
| Brand ID | 00954 |
| Alias | Sugar |
| Country | United States |
| Residence | The Bowery, New York |
| Birth Name | Willem Bernard Floures |

Won **52** (KO 12) + Lost **4** (KO 2) + Drawn **0** = **56**

# THE LAUGHTER I HEAR

I can take a punch. That used to be the problem. Twelve rounds without so much as a knockdown, or getting numb at the knees, tends to bore the audience. It bore right into the audience's attention span, splitting it in half. I gave them ten seconds at the start of my career. At best one of my fights rendered them five.

Five seconds.

If I don't make it count, they watch the other guy, who does everything I do, but maybe a little bit better. If you asked me, I'd agree:

## ACCURATE STATEMENT

But, yeah, I can take a punch. The problem then is when I start to feel those hooks to the body, the punches right against my shoulders. I shouldn't feel those; I am conditioned to embrace the impact and go searching with the jab, jab, jab, jab, even if they only end up hitting air, jab, jab, waiting for the moment I can launch a power shot left right where it counts.

If I can take a punch, they can take a punch.

## IT STILL HURTS

I give them my best and at the very least they might take a step back, shake off the hook, the uppercut to the chin.

Maybe a knockdown, four count, if I'm lucky.

If it's me that's hitting the canvas, it takes me three just to get my old tired ass off the ground, another four to get up to my feet. The referees with their endless commentaries—

"Are you okay?!"

"Can you see me?!"

"Look into my eyes!"
"Follow my nose!"
Does very little to reassure me.

How many times have I hit the canvas at the expense of myself but to bolster what this is, the betterment of the brand?

## ARE YOU ASKING?

Lately it's been a lot.
So what I'm saying is—

## I COULD TAKE A PUNCH

Nowadays every punch feels like glass cutting skin, earth quaking up my spine, calling me collect, telling me to stay down.

## END IT NOW

I've got a few fights left in me, thank you.

Thank you everyone, my would-be fans, people that used to bet their holiday bonuses on me, the penultimate of the name everyone couldn't help but stop and watch whenever we fought.

## 'SUGAR' WILLEM FLOURES

That's a name I built from the ground up. I wasn't the first to systematically climb the ranks, beating the sugar out of everyone I had known to be inferior, leaving only the sour taste of defeat, my claim forever being:

"I am the greatest!"

I can still hear it now. In the silence of this locker room, blood drying on my face, I can still hear those words.

And I was. I was the greatest.

## IS
## WAS
## WILL BE
## TWO OF THESE SIMPLY WILL NOT DO

But the most appropriate might be the least flattering. Past tense.

I *was* 'Sugar' Willem Floures.

I had mastered it all, the ins and outs of what I could do to beat myself up. I had everything under control. My demons, my weaknesses, my vices, my tendency to lose track of time, all of it was under control.

I could take it on at a second's notice, some wide-eyed newcomer thinking he's got it all down, what it means to be me, calling me out, challenging me like this is some game and not the sweet science, but you know what? I always did. I fought cold, straight, no training. I used to be able to see every single punch, bob, weave, flick of the cheek, squint of the eye, long before they'd ever register.

Now, this blood as evidence of my defeat, they see the very same in me.

## I USED TO BE ABLE TO TAKE A PUNCH

I have never been able to take defeat. And when I didn't see that punch coming, I swallowed the blood alongside the painful realization that maybe, just maybe, I forgot what it means to fight.

## I AM FORGETTING MYSELF

How difficult it is to climb to your feet when rocked, stunned, trying to beat the ten count only to go back to doing your best not to be beaten to the punch yet again by someone thinking they've got it right, me, everything from strategy to street cred.

I hate the way it feels, a trickle of blood slowly dripping down your forehead. I thought the wound had healed. Guess not.

Wipe it away quick enough to feel the warm liquid grow cold.

It is starting to swell up.

The welt will be big enough to be unforgettable.

Spencer is going to take a picture of it. I know he is.

He'll never let it go, this loss. My first loss in the last five fights.

What he doesn't understand is how hard I fought only to barely win by decision. When you win you always remember the cheers of the audience; when you lose you try your damnedest to erase the sneers and laughter they send in your direction. No one is able to completely remove the mark a loss leaves on your psyche much less the scars that show in the faintest of light.

I used to be able to take a punch, now all I seem to do is take on losses.

## FIGHT RECORD

Okay, look, let me say something about my record. Don't think I'm narcissistic because I am not (at least I don't think I am). I have a good record.

You can say that "Ironman" did well to spread the Floures name with his attempted suicide and bout with depression, one of the biggest national stories in recent sports history, but I was the one Williem Floures that created this whole league, made it so that the name Floures is synonymous with combat, with boxing.

## FIFTY-TWO WINS

Might as well be a fine wine because thinking about it makes me feel all warm and buzzed.

## TWELVE BY KO

I managed that not because they couldn't take a punch—they can take a punch as well as I can—but because of wearing them down first with the jab. Like Spencer always said, lead with the jab, smother with the jab, and wait for the opening. Land as close to the temple or as snugly under the chin and rock that brain, send them to the canvas, watch them dance their way to defeat. I waited them out, knowing that I'd get impatient.

"Fight like you are not who you are and that'll keep them on their toes."

## WISE WORDS

Spencer, my trainer and agent, I couldn't have amassed the record without his guidance. He's right though—
I know how they'll fight just like they know how I'll fight.
They know what I'm thinking.
I know what they are thinking.
We are alike because we are alike.
So to win, to be the best, I can't be myself.
I must fight like I'm someone else, like I don't know what I'm doing.
Worked for the majority of my wins, not so much for the four losses.
But I don't like to talk about that. Means Spencer always talks about it. Means it's something that I should do because I wouldn't normally do it myself. Go against the grain, the expected.

## FOUR LOSSES

Not so bad.

## MAKE IT FIVE

Still not bad.

## IT IS BAD
## I'M JUST NOT GOING TO ADMIT IT
## UNTIL I HAVE TO

Here's the rationalization that works best:
It benefits one it benefits all. Younger throws the shot and I, the older, take it. I hit the canvas. I taste copper. Sure, sure, I look bad but it's getting better. The audience gets a knockdown. We both get purse money.
He'll go out after this, night on the town, while I go to the

7

emergency room, welts the size of a second head swelling from the side of my face.

That's my rationalization and I'm going to stick to it.

I'm going to keep applying pressure to the wound on my forehead and I'm not going to look in any mirrors.

I don't want to see what I look like.

I can feel the welt on the side of my face throbbing. It must be the size of a baseball. I can get past most of the loss but it's what they do to drain the welt that I associate most with my current situation.

Proof that I'm not a narcissist:

## I ADMIT IT

I admit it, okay?

I admit that I'm getting old.

I should think about retiring. I really should.

If I do, that means…it means the worst for what I wanted out of this life. You step aside. Retirement is about as punishing an act as it sounds; you retire all cred; you are incapable of climbing into the ring, between the ropes, never again able to wear the gloves, bite deep into the mouth guard, stare yourself down across the ring, fighting not only yourself but everything you don't see boiling to the surface.

No matter what their alias might be, they are all me.

We are all alike.

And no one will take the place of 'Sugar' Willem Floures.

If I retired, though, how would I be able to protect my record? My legacy? My name? This brand? Can they really have the brand in their best interests? It's too easy to be forgotten in this world.

## BRAND AWARENESS

Willem Floures is synonymous with the sport.

However, it might not be in a few short years.

There are plenty of other names fighting, all of them trying to book the same stadiums, secure the same Pay Per View slots, that Floures has successfully achieved in the four and a half decades of fight that I've championed. All of us in the league, we fight each other as much as we fight the world. The world might not care for much longer. That's what bleeds the most, hurts the deepest: The thought that every punch landed, every punch absorbed, every scar carved into my skin, will be as insignificant as the dead buried six feet under, aging stone slabs the only real remembrance, their only real legacy.

## I AM AFRAID OF IT

What I worry most is that my time in the ring is passing, slipping from my grip.

## THE LAUGHTER

Looking back all I hear is laughter. All I see is white. All I taste is the ache of my bleeding mouth, tongue numb, my eyes wanting so very much to roll back, have a look at the inside of my broken skull.

Looking ahead, all I hear is Spencer.

"Before I send you to the hospital to lick those poor little wounds of yours, we have to go through this!"

Just his way: tough, stern, uncompromising.

I can barely sit up straight but he's throwing a screen in my face, pointing at the fight footage fresh from the feed.

I always wonder how Spencer can afford every little new gadget in the world but then again I forget that Floures is a moneymaker of a name.

Haven't spent a dime myself, but that's because I'm not in this for the money. I'm in this for—

Well if I said it I wouldn't believe it.

People step in the ring to fight themselves.

That's the plain truth. No doubt about it.

"Round two you got it all wrong! What the hell were you thinking?! Did you not hear me say duck the left hook? 'Executioner' uses the left hook as much as you fucking did back when you were ten fights into your career. How could you forget?!"

That's another problem:

## FORGETTING

My memory. It's not what it used to be. I have a lot of bad habits, many of them I have no recollection of and it probably makes me look horrible.

I tend to apologize as much as I thank the fans.

"Left hook, left hook, left hook! Round five you're all over the place!"

Spencer pauses the footage and points to where I stick my chin out like an amateur, getting caught with an uppercut that resulted in the first of two knockdowns.

"Yeah well at least I get up after this one," the best excuse I can make.

Spencer does that thing where his right eye closes and he shakes his head. Something only Spencer Mullen would do, his way of dealing with smart-ass remarks (my forte).

"Round eight flatline!"

"I know, I know."

"You 'know,' but you don't understand! How *does* the man carrying the legendary name of 'Sugar' get caught with such plain shots to the face? Why the hell were you not covering your face?!"

Spencer fast forwards the footage to where I foolishly drop my arms, making it look like a taunt, when in fact it was because I felt the tickle, the feeling of goose bumps, going up both of my arms. I was gassed.

Completely gassed.

If I bothered to block, much less throw another punch, it could have been swatting a fly. And the fly would get away without a single mark.

"It helps the brand," another smartass remark.

Spencer taps at the screen, bringing up one of the countless fight reports, checks the CompuBox, number of punches landed versus thrown, and doesn't say a word. He looks up at me, eye closed, a sigh, and taps the screen.

Yes, I get it.

This wasn't just a loss.

It may very well have been a turning point.

'X' won, 11-0 record. Ten by KO.

## DECENT FIGHT RECORD

Is he a prodigy? You might say he is.

"You'll want to take him up on the rematch clause," Spencer insists.

A rematch. What does it mean when I go pale, flush with fear, at such a thought? Don't answer that. Spencer leans in close and looks at the welt.

Makes a clicking noise with his tongue, "This was the left hook that done it."

Yeah, it was. And it probably hurts. I just don't feel it yet.

Adrenaline hasn't fully flushed from my system yet.

Once it does, I better be on the painkillers.

"Just get me to the hospital," I say.

He pulls back, crosses his arms and shakes his head: "Tell me first, what is it that you're fighting for?"

I lower my head, no reply.

"It must be something because it used to be for you. You fought to fight yourself. When you were two and zero, fresh out, you told me you wanted to fight to be the best you could possibly be. Now I look at you and I see someone bruised up and broken, looking to blow it all."

He grabs my forearm, my hands still wrapped in tape, "What. Are. You. Fighting. For?"

I look at my taped up hands.

I look down at the blue gloves hanging slack against the side of a nearby bench. I look at the locker room door, open ajar, not a single invading source, typically we'd have to keep it closed, locked, because every media personality would be clawing at the door, finding a way in, wanting a sound bite, something, anything, but now, I see an empty hall and the lingering nuance of stale laughter. At my expense, at my loss.

I look up at Spencer, the only person that cares about who I am, rather than who I fought so hard to be, and I...

I can't.

I have no answer to that question.

Likely the most important question to be posed at this point of my life and career and I haven't a clue.

I have lost focus, lost favor.

"I can't answer that question."

Spencer relents, but still manages a sigh that digs under my skin.

"Let's get you to a hospital. God forbid you'd want to *feel* the magnitude of your decisions."

He's right. I'm quick to act but last to understand the effects of what I've done. By the time you read any of what I've said, I will have yet to fully comprehend the telling. I might tell you everything, more than I want to tell, and it won't hit me as reality for weeks, months; it might never register as reality. That's another scar on the surface of my being:

Incapable of keeping private and public life apart.

I don't know how much they know about me.

They probably know the whole story.

You probably already know what's going to happen.

You know where this is going, right?

Wish you could point me in the right direction.

## LAUGHTER
## A CHUCKLE

Not quite cheery, more like the clearing of one's throat. A sweet feminine voice, made to be sweet because it's her duty to take care of me. Nurse of many, nurse of few, tends to my wounds while holding my hand, checking my pulse, scribbling notes onto my chart.

How am I doing?

I'm on painkillers.

Right about now, I'm doing swell. If you're asking about later, we don't talk about later. We let everything that isn't the dozy trance of "right now" slip by as nonessential.

The nurse notices that I'm awake, "How are they treating you?"

By "they" she means the pills.

"Swell," I reply, slurring the word so that it sounds more like "*shwellp*."

"Oh boy you don't need any more."

No I don't.

But she gets me feeling good, asking me if I feel this, feel that, scribbling more onto my chart.

I do my best to strike up a conversation, "I used to go twelve rounds and still have enough energy to hit the bars for another twelve!"

That's what I said. I can't be sure it's actually what she heard.

Again, the painkillers.

She smiles and giggles because that's what she does, as part of her 'cute nurse' routine. Says something like, "A lesser man would have tapped out."

Whatever that means.

I just don't want her to keep scribbling in my chart.

"I used to see that left hook from a mile away. I used to be the one that threw the hook just so that they'd see it coming and duck. I used it to get them into a position where I could land an uppercut right under the chin. Left hook, left hook, pause, assess, uppercut while they block, block, weave, duck, impact."

"My my," pandering, being nice, because, why not?

"Those were the days when I could really throw a punch. Never went down though, never got them down to the canvas for more than a five count. Power but I have a chin. Had a chin. Cast-iron, I'd say. Now I can hear glass shatter whenever I take one to the jaw."

More scribbling, not really listening, but the nurse is nice enough and who really listens to anyone anyway?

"I'm 'Sugar' Willem Floures. Got to mean something right?"

The nurse nods, "My mom used to watch every single one of your fights. She always bet on Sugar."

"What about you?"

Not understanding my slurred speech, she seems to say, "You had one of the best win-streaks I've ever seen."

Again I ask, "What about you?"

"Me? Oh I always bet on the other guy."

She looks at me, must have some kind of grimace on my face because she chooses to explain herself, "Don't get me wrong; I love watching a good Floures fight but I always bet on the underdog. I watched every fight hoping that you'd surprise yourself, catch one and go down for the knockout."

"Then tonight's fight was good then?"

Oh, now she hears me loud and clear. "If you want me to be honest, yes—I enjoyed the fight. Executioner looks just like you when you were just starting out and the league fights were in those high school stadiums and broadcast on cable TV."

I want to defend myself but my guard is already down and the nurse managed to jab her way right into the most fragile depths of my ego.

Not that there's a whole lot left to maintain.

I go quiet. She continues scribbling into the chart and for a brief moment I consider what she might be writing down, what must be so important that she sacrifices legibility for the speed of the scribble?

## IS MY CONDITION REALLY THAT BAD?

There's something I don't want to think about right now, not while I'm on so much medication. Think about the wrong thing and it becomes all you can think about. So I'm thinking instead about what I might do as a counter, saying something that will somehow make her regret her choice to cheer for 'Executioner.'

I garble my words, not quite sure what I'm trying to say, when Spencer walks into the hospital room, instructing the nurse to leave.

"Yes, sir, I must keep a log of—"

"That can happen later. He'll be here all night."

Spencer glares at the nurse. She looks at me, "You feel better, okay?" and quickly leaves the room. Door squeaks shut.

Spencer pulls a chair up to the left side of the hospital bed.

Sits down and leans forward, "Don't you talk to anyone. How many times have I told you, huh?"

I close my eyes, letting the nameless force pull me under, into a deep sleep more preferable than listening to yet another lecture, but Spencer's voice cuts deep enough to sever that tether, and I rise back up, eyes opening, looking, focusing, Spencer asking me what I told the nurse.

"Nothing, just good times."

"Good times? That won't cut it. What did you tell her?"

I take a moment to recall what I had said.

Sure, fine, I tell him. You don't need to hear it a second time.

Spencer shakes his head, "You never learn do you? Do not talk to anyone when you are under the influence *of anything*." A younger version of me would ask why.

For Spencer's sake, he doesn't manage a younger version.

He's stuck with old and busted.

Old and busted he can deal with.

Doze through the lecture, about how I am susceptible to disclosure of information that could leak to the media, ruining the prefight promotional junkets, which is, according to Spencer (really, according to anyone but me; I loathe it; loathe it all), the *fight before the fight*.

## THE LECTURE

Lecture about how a match is divided into two, maybe three if you count the post-fight conference.

**1)** The interviews, the meet-and-greets, the spotlights on sparring, method, strategy; the celebrity mingling, etc.

**2)** The actual fight, the fight that I thought this was really all about but I guess not; more and more these days it seems like this is an afterthought. Who really trains anymore?

**3)** That post-fight conference where the media grills you on your performance, like anyone really needs that after going twelve rounds.

On and on and on he'll go and I need to follow him, agreeing at the end of every sentence.

## THIS IS HOW IT GOES
## KEY ELEMENTS TO A PROFFESSIONAL FIGHT

But it goes, and eventually he will stop.

Things settle down and I get to enjoy a brief but lovely period of recuperation.

That is, unless Spencer *doesn't stop* and proceeds to tell me:

"And you're good for it."

"Huh?" Good for what?

I already know, and I can feel that knot of dread already forming, twisting, coiling up, somewhere deep in my stomach.

"Executioner v. Sugar II. I signed the contract. Word should be reaching the media..." he looks at his wrist, not that he ever wore a watch, "right about *now*." Stops, looks around the hospital for the first time, and then asks me, "Excited?"

Excited is not the word.

I let the effects of the painkillers pull me back under in the nonsense of a drug-laced consciousness. Temporary escape.

Last thing I hear before completely letting go, falling into a coma-like sleep, is Spencer saying, "Let's get you well. Got to get you back on the routine in a week's time."

But I am not there.

Partial consciousness. I play with the prospect of never resurfacing.

I will comb the *nonspace* and turn it into my home.

## HOME SWEET HOME

I'll be right here. Fine.

But loose escapes are little more than lingering.

Ask Spencer and he'd say it's not far off from loathing.

I just want to sleep.

These days I fail to fend off the hours that used to be mine; I wake when I wake, frantically rising to my feet when I discover that I slept through to beyond the point where the day can be anything more than half of an afternoon. And the routine, it places me to the side of myself, incapable of keeping track of anything else but the pressures of every incoming promotional event. They all ask me:

"What does it mean to be Willem Floures?"

I had a statement prepared, but I must have left it behind, somewhere, maybe resting on a table somewhere.

Yawn and let it take me, for now, the drugged sleep.
I'd like to ask them the same question.
I'd like to reply by saying:
"You tell me."
All I know is that I'm not the same person I used to be.

## EXECUTIONER V. SUGAR II...

I signed the contract...
Word should be reaching the media right about *now*...
Excited?
Hear gasps, deep breaths.
Familiar, they are my breaths.
Tired, strained.
Let's get you well...
Got to get you back on the routine in a week's time...

## THE ROUTINE

I can't get back to myself, much less the day-to-day.
"Sugar, what happened back there? It appeared as though
he gassed you by focusing on body shots. Would you say that's
accurate?"
Don't ask me.
Ask one of *them*.
They know me better than I know myself.

# THE LAUGHTER I FEAR

## AUDIENCE LAUGHTER

Still have the scars on my face, the loose tooth in my mouth, the jitters so I have to hide my hands from the cameras. Anyway, it's back to the routine.

The talk of every day until it happens is:

## EXECUTIONER VS. SUGAR II

It used to be the other way around:

## SUGAR VS. EXECUTIONER

*What does it feel like to be the challenger?*
That's a question I've already been asked.

It's a knockout of a question, first of many. Good thing Spencer sits at my side, different because most agents stay behind the scenes. Not Spencer.

He's always been right there.

Field these questions, man. Please. Go right ahead.

I tongue the open laceration on the inside of my cheek. It's the wound that wouldn't heal quick enough. The mouth guard fell out of my mouth, Executioner failing to land a shot but no matter because I managed to clench my jaw, grind my teeth into the soft gummy tissue before the referee stopped the fight so that I might replace the mouth guard.

Memory.

Memory I'd rather forget.

Memory, a memory that is not a part of the media junket.

## AUDIENCE LAUGHTER

What are they laughing at?

Oh it's something Spencer said. Good of him to speak for me—

"Well then, last week's fight is history and if I do say so myself it was a piece of history. The world saw the end of Sugar's long-running win streak against what the media had called, in the weeks prior to fight night, a prodigy, a new era for Floures."

Spencer the expert agent and publicist replies, "What's the question?"

Thing about daytime talk shows is they tend to sensationalize and place opinion on the public. It is whatever their audience wants. Get them laughing, get them interested. As long as you *get them*, the truth and/or value of the coverage is less important.

The host winks, gloats, gets to the point:

"Will Sugar be ready for X this time?"

See what I mean?

They could care less about the harmful emotional effect of their questions; this is about entertainment.

Spencer ducks the question, retaliating with a bluff, "Every fight counts for something, I assure you. It is not that we aren't ready for the fight; every professional is ready to exercise his or her craft. Every boxer fights with the sweet science in mind. Sugar is no different."

"I am not denying that to be the case, Mr. Mullen, but the world wants to know if Sugar will be ready to face himself or will it be another blunder of a match?"

Relentless.

## WOULD EXPECT NOTHING LESS

It doesn't seem to faze Spencer though.

"What do you want to hear? You ask and I speak the truth. In specifics, I am confident enough to tell you that we have examined Executioner's preferred strategics, where he's coming from as a strategist, and everyone," turns to the audience, the cameras, points at random faces, "every one of you should know that Sugar sees the math, the strategy, the one-two-duck-hook-low; Sugar used to fight like this. Let's not kid ourselves. He's got more experience than the entire league of them. He's used to battling himself, be it 'Ice,' 'Breakneck,' 'Kid KO,' or, the 'Executioner.' They are just names, aliases; faces in the dirt of each step. Sugar has the record to prove that he knows every strength, knows every weakness. He understands their round-by-round strategy. A decade ago Sugar and I created it from the ground up, working in subtle psychology into the sweet science."

Weigh in that answer.

See what the host has for us next.

## COMMERICAL BREAK

Of course, to distill and strip away the bulk of Spencer's reply, they cut to commercial. They want to focus on the negative rather than the positive. It's what the audience wants. Drama, the dish, new shocking information to please.

## DISAPPOINTED

They are disappointed in me.

I am disappointed in myself.

The host tells us, "Okay, I understand that it is in your best interest to maintain Sugar's persona as it once was in a positive light; however, the light is no longer lime and it is no longer looking for you. It is in *our* best interest to paint the picture of a true loss. We get the audience to believe it and it makes for a better story."

The host looks at me, "Win the rematch and you recoup not only what you lost but also double what you put into this. It's your career, your identity, your life that's on the line. It is in our *best interest* to pave the way for a comeback."

## BEST INTEREST

This is not good.

Spencer is offended by the host's tone. He is silent, brooding, listening, acting the part, acting as if he agrees.

## AND WE'RE BACK
## AUDIENCE LAUGHTER
## FAKE
## ON COMMAND

"We are back with none other than 'Sugar' Willem Floures, one of the greatest fighters of all time."

Spencer mutters under his breath, "He *is* the greatest fighter of all time…"

More talk about the loss, *that* loss, and how 'Executioner' was faster, more agile, capable of outpunching and outmaneuvering me around the ring.

"Might this be why you chose to stay on the ropes?"

Spencer answers, "It's called rope-a-dope, a valid technique. It is how we stole three rounds on the cards from 'Executioner.'"

"That very well may be the case but between the use of lateral movement to duck the mids, Executioner landed," the host reads from one of his notecards, ninety-one percent of punches to the face. This is not healthy for a fighter your age, Sugar. We worry about the lasting damage one fight can do to your reflexes, your ability to defend yourself."

I open my mouth to speak but Spencer beats me to it:

"We have released the medical reports to the press. He received only minor injuries, nothing a single night's stay in the hospital couldn't treat."

The host looks at me.

Says, "He looks pretty rough."

I reply, "It was a rough fight."

## AND THAT'S SOMETHING

And that's something the host wants to hear.

And that's something Spencer will lecture me about afterwards.

Addressing me, the host asks, "Did you see the punch coming?"

Spencer with the save, "Most knockouts are flash, blind, quick and to the temple, under the chin, somewhere where the body is rendered useless. If I were to hit you in the temple lightly right now, you would get dizzy, feel slightly nauseous; hell, that might be enough to knock you out."

"Mr. Mullen, are you threatening me?"

Every media venue and their propensity for controversy…

But Spencer said it for a reason. He must have.

He's way too good to get caught up in the nonessentials of a slanderous interview.

"Threats are of everyday life. In the context of the rematch, the threat here is not what Sugar lost—not at all—the threat is in what 'Executioner' stands to lose."

The host cocks his head to the side, "Interesting take." Again he turns his attention to me. Predictable. Most venues seek to speak to me directly rather than through Spencer's testimonies.

"What's your take on this, Sugar?"

Like trying to gain approval from someone's mother, the host holds up both hands, indication of fair play, "That is if I may speak to the man himself?"

Spencer and I realize that we are at that point of the interview.

I need to say something.

They need to hear my voice, need to make sure that I'm responsive. Most of all, they just want to know something about what I'm not.

Fielding for new gossip, new rumor.

"You are talking to him right now," Spencer comments.


AUDIENCE LAUGHTER

Seems to get the audience's attention.

I don't find it very funny myself but that's not up to me.

I take the punches.

I take the onslaught.

Everything else I try my best to let it wash over me, unaffected.

Host readies the pounce—

He gets at least one question, one question before the opportunity spoils. What's it going to be?

What do you think?

## WAIT FOR IT…

*"Do you think it's time to retire?"*
I wait for it too.
It doesn't register at first. Spencer gives me this look like I'm ruining it, really smearing the interview, fucking it up for myself by being slow with my reply…but he's right and it doesn't hit me at first.
Slow crawl.
One of those straights that pushes through your gloves, causing your gloves to shoot back towards you and away, parting the sea as the powerful strike lands right on the nose.
Those kinds of punches you can only see in slow motion.
When it lands, there's little more than a tickle. It starts at the point of impact, the bridge of the nose. Feel it like an insect's legs on bare skin as it crawls up your arm or back. Feel it as it expands, impact warm and the dots, they swarm your vision until you don't see much of anything.
If you're lucky you are still standing, still fighting back.

## FIGHT, FIGHT, FIGHT

But lately I haven't been up on luck.
Like right now, when I answer honestly, an answer right from the gut, I don't mean it to come out the way it does.
I say:
"I think so."
What I really mean is—

## I THINK SO BUT I DON'T THINK I'M READY

I have a whole lot left to prove.
I still don't fully understand myself.
I have to keep fighting to find myself.
Got to try to remember why I fought in the first place.
Why I was always so hard on myself.
Quick to scrutinize and analyze and obsess.

## TOO LATE

The headline most recognized when associated with my name.

Poor choices are plain and simple in the past tense.

I can see them and understand why I made such a bad decision; however, it never shows. It never reads *you are going to regret it*, until it's too late.

## TOO LATE

*Read*: I didn't mean to do and/or say whatever I did, whatever I said.

Spencer on the recovery.

Wish he could take a punch or two for me. Even with a good chin, even with the gloved up hands, the cushioning and conditioning, those damn things still hurt. Like right now, I feel like someone's punched me.

Dazed and confused look on my face…

And I hear what I fear most.

## AUDIENCE LAUGHTER

This is why Spencer usually does all the talking.

I won't be able to take that one back.

This is the laughter I fear most.

## AUDIENCE LAUGHTER

They are laughing at me, and we all know it—the people in attendance, the people watching at home. X and his camp.

Everyone was listening as I said it. You don't come back from something like this. It's out there, in the open, material like getting stunned by a haymaker punch; I have to be extra careful, guarding every action, every idea, every step, until I shake free of the humiliation.

*Humiliation hurts more than any swift strike to the stomach.*

You can absorb those with a clench of the abdominal muscles, letting muscle protect ribcage and organs from the impact, but something like this, words said that cannot be unsaid, are beyond protection.

They exist, hanging there.

Hear it?

## AUDIENCE LAUGHTER

I am stunned.

I fear it. I am afraid, but I cannot let it show or else it will be far worse than I would ever be willing to face.

The audience is my opponent.

The audience looks nothing like me.

Do I have room to say anything else?

I probably shouldn't.

Clam up, sweating, looking down at the mug full of water.

Wait until it ends. Ignore the host's voice.

Spencer, say what you need to say.

I won't be saying another word.

## CARE TO EXPLAIN...

Three words from the host's mouth that slip through my defenses.

It gets me to thinking:

If they want my defeat this early in the prefight festivities, the long routine of venue to venue, meet and greet and gloating, I have one thing to say:

Why am I the main guest of this show?

Why am I the guest if they want me to grovel?

Why do they see me as this, when I still have a few fights left in me?

I want to fight.

I need to fight.

I feel like I've lost a part of myself that I need to fight to get back.

## AUDIENCE LAUGHTER

Why don't I tell them that?

Yeah, but it's too late.

Spencer explains our basic strategy, something we shouldn't really talk about but because I said something I shouldn't have, he is doing his best to cover up the error. It's not like it's a strategy I'd use anyway.

He's just pulling something out of the air, pure hot air.

## BASIC STRATEGY,
## ACCORDING TO SPENCER MULLEN:

1) Keep your form tight, punches sharper but not necessarily cast in power. Too many power shots gasses you early.

2) Hydrated before, during, and after fight—a cup of water every hour at the very least.

3) Emphasis on shorter hooks and uppercuts leading with, of course, the jab. The slower the punch, the harder the impact. Sit on your punches whenever necessary; power shots used sparingly.

4) Can't stress it enough—lead with the jab. Long jabs rather than short create distance and control. Save short jabs for testing the waters, searching and sifting for an opportunity.

5) Focus on chopping the opponent down to size by working the body. Jab to the head, right hook to the body—a sound two-hit lead on a potential flurry of shots.

6) Flurries should be at most four shots. Odds are only half will connect; rest are at the expense of landing at least one. Most flurries work against conserving energy; use sparingly.

7) Remember that every punch is about creating an opportunity, identifying your opponent's weak spots, and consistently going for the body.

8) Fight conservatively while avoiding excessive defense; that ploy tends to work against you on the judges' cards.

9) Establish your ground and keep it; no backpedaling.

10) Time your punches right and you can block a punch with another punch.

## AUDIENCE'S ATTENTION SPAN

Satiate the masses, the audience. The host nods and turns to the camera, "There you have it: Straight from the source, we have a sound strategy and one hell of a fight to look forward to."

There will be a fight, sure, but will it consist of looking forward or looking back? I see X and he reminds me of how fast on my feet I had been before hitting thirty.

Looking forward is the same as looking back.

If I fight the past, I wonder if I can improve the future.

## AUDIENCE APPLAUSE

Spencer waits until we are back in the dressing room to call me out on yet another error.

That error, yes, and I deserve it.

Not going to let you hear what he said but, more or less, he says what he always says—one eye closed, sighing, shaking his head, mid-shout he discusses how it makes me look. Fodder, more fuel for the promo machine.

I could explain myself but he's not looking for explanations; Spencer explains how my comment is already spreading like wildfire, trending across social media sources; they have a snippet of the interview where I look like I'm under the influence of some kind of medication. Superimposed are my words, I THINK SO, in bold white. Five-second intervals repeated, I THINK SO.

I look like a wreck.

## I THINK SO

Spencer explains how it'll take two weeks to get this meme to die.

"Another fight we don't need!"

And another thing he makes sure I recognize after every interview, every forsaken media spectacle, "It took us ten years to get them used to having me in the spotlight with you, holding your hand like you can't think for yourself!"

Progress made seemingly shatters with a single error.

## I THINK SO

It lingers like a stillborn thought.

And then Spencer repeats, "I think so!" in unison with the echo localized in my mind.

I hear it even though it's no longer mine to have.

I fucked up. Yeah, I get it.

It's just another fight, after all.

Spencer shouts, "What the hell is wrong with you, Willem?"

If I told him the truth, what I really fear, he would join in on the laughter. If I told him the truth, what I really want to do, he would figure me for an ungrateful client. He used to treat me like an equal, a friend; these days I will admit to having fallen off, momentum lost.

He carries me.

I used to carry him.

"I'm tired," is all I tell him. Not quite an excuse but not far off either.

I can hear the audience...

## AUDIENCE LAUGHTER

I wonder if they are laughing with or at the guest.

There is wonder in the fact that they can forget the greatest news bites but fail to let something like I THINK SO go.

Negativity floats.

The positive swims for a second before swallowing too much seawater, and down it goes, to the very bottom of the sea.

I'd like to live there.

Think about it—down there, where no human being can subsist—I'd like to fight the ocean, the tides; I'd like to face myself in the mirror and see me for who I am now, not what I used to be.

A fighter loses the fight and it's a slippery slope to rock bottom.

Can I hit rock bottom?

Can I live there?

## NO

Spencer claps his hands together, "Hey!"

"Yeah…?"

Look at me. I must look like hell, pre-defeated before the prefight can even begin. Embarrassing.

"You say you're tired well good because we have Bedside Chat next."

I knew it was coming.

I'm not sure I'm ready yet.

But I don't tell Spencer this. I keep it to myself.

Instead I ask, "What about training? I feel weak…I need to recondition myself for this fight."

"We'll get to that," Spencer replies, waving his hand in the air, dismissing my query.

I need to hit the heavy bag, need to work the snap back into my jab.

Over the last couple years, I've barely trained at all.

Spencer with a poetic excuse, "Every step you take is a training exercise, now come on, let's get going. We *cannot* be late to any scheduled press event. That's the last thing we need, to be marked 'LOP' for the rematch."

He means guests marked "LOP" are unpredictable and are known to skip events and/or crash events. You might as well not even go than be late to the junket. And if we were late, Spencer would say the same thing.

He'd tell the cabbie to turn around, sacrificing that event while we make our way to the next one, early.

Sure the excuse is good enough but that doesn't make it true.

Training involves heart rate, toning, recuperation.

Most of the prefight window I'm staring into a camera, being criticized or considered a spectacle, an unfortunate celebrity.

I can't say it ever was very exciting…

But maybe.

X seems to enjoy it, which means, well yeah, I must have liked all the attention too.

"Once upon a time."

"What?"

I shake my head, "Nothing."

"Well come on, hustle Will!"

Up and out of the dressing room, sprinting down the hall. Here we are, yet again, how many times have we done this?

Even if I knew I'd still find reason enough to forget.

Wish I could have selected what to keep versus what to forget.

I listen to the distant audience laughter as we step out into the back alley of the studio building.

I practice my introduction on the cabbie. Unresponsive, the cabbie takes a drag from his cigarette and says, "You're that fighter."

Yes, I am.

Whatever that means.

Label me a fighter.

How does that help define who I am?

## INTRODUCTION
## READ: I AM TRYING

The cabbie doesn't give a name and there's nothing left to say. Spencer gives the cabbie directions.

The rest is silence, and I am still staring into the rearview mirror, watching the disinterest hang over the cabbie's face, gloom of a near-frown, stench of long hours sitting and smoking, wrinkles forming where it counts most, reminding me of my own age.

And how old I have become...

I am a fighter. *Edit*: I am an old fighter.

I am a fighter that doesn't know when to quit.

## EDIT: I AM STILL TRYING

I think I am, anyway.

Got to be something worth fighting for, right?

# THE LAUGHTER MOST DEAR

Just now I remembered this one training exercise that I created, without anyone else's help, not even Spencer, who is the king of coming up with creative forms of punishment; it was this simple little stunt where you merge between five to eight rounds of sparring with a jog around the ring. Each round is split down the middle so that the first minute of the first round, you spar; the last minute of the first round, you jog around the ring. You reverse it for round two, jogging in the first minute and sparring in the last, back and forth until you are gassed. When you are gassed, you spar one last round, but not before chugging straight vodka from the bottle right before manning the gloves.

I did this not because it helped me physically (maybe it did, don't know) but because it helped so much mentally, just being able to compress all of it into one forty-five minute training session.

Time is "of the essence" and even back then I knew that I only had so much of it reserved for the gym. Over the course of my entire career, I got the sense that very little of training consisted of conditioning the body.

Mostly we went to public places and made sure people, fans, haters, whoever it might have been, were there to watch.

I get the sense that I can measure time not in hours but in media junkets. Like this one, Bedside Chat, where I lie down on one bed facing away from the other bed where X will lay, we compete against each other in rehearsed sketches facilitated by a central computer programmer.

The world watches our words type out on a screen that we cannot see.

Via an earpiece in our right ear, we hear the producers telling us what to type next. What I love the most about this is how we receive notice from the listeners, the viewers, the audience, the world.

Not a sound.

Never a sound.

Instead we see their commentaries as a trickle of type, just like ours only smaller, set in italics, running across the bottom of the screen only they can see.

We see it later, after the event is over.

Post-criticism, it feels so much better, easier to handle; Bedside Chat started as a feature on a blog and has now become a celebrity mainstay.

## CANDID

That's the word used in the Chat tagline.

Not far from the truth. If only the world knew that everything was rehearsed, prewritten, and really what X and I do is attempt to be ourselves.

Be *me*.

I worry that I'll get that part wrong.

I think I'm confident but I can't be sure.

Maybe I'm self-conscious. Have I always been self-conscious?

## CHAT PROMPT

The way this looks, both beds are cast in synthetic moonlight. X might as well not even be here; I don't see him walk in just as he doesn't see me. I type out what I'm supposed to type out:

## HELLO

But that's not enough, the producer voice speaks into my ear via the provided earpiece, so I opt for:

## HI WILLEM FLOURES HERE, THANKS FOR HAVING ME

X types out:

## GREETINGS WILLEM FLOURES HERE SWINGING HAYMAKERS AND HAVING A HELL OF A TIME

I quickly get the sense of competition, what sort of competition this is going to be. My word against his, his word against mine. Who will they believe? What will they have us do? I'm kind of glad that Spencer was forced to stay back. Everything that happens now is:

### CANDID

And by that I am certain.

### I THINK SO

Please let that die.

Producer voice in my ear tells me that I'm going to say something about the last fight. I say something about the last fight, just that it was a good one, and that I know we can both do better next time. The producer whines, wanting more from me than that, so he offers a prompt for both of us. The audience can see the prompt:

### A LITTLE BIT ABOUT YOURSELF: HOW DID YOU COME UP WITH THE "ONE-TWO SOUTHPAW SLIP?"

A signature punch of mine. I'm happy to talk about it extensively. So what exactly do they want?

I explain as clearly as I can how it consists of leading in orthodox, standard positioning, leading with a left jab, jab, jab, jab, wait and feel it out for the switch-footing to southpaw, throwing a right hook to the body, another jab to the face, as I do; the meat of the move is in the left straight to the body, sometimes I aim for the face, which, when landed, provides enough power to stun. I know because that's probably how I was KOed last fight.

Right?

Wrong it seems.

I get this wrong.

That is not the "One-Two Southpaw Slip."

The producer voice speaks into my ear, curious about what the hell I'm talking about when X is evidently the one that's correct.

I know what I know which alarms me when, considering my position here, I am prone to questions about my life, my boxing style.

If I get it wrong, what does that mean for me?

Does it make me any less than I already am?

## DID YOU REALLY VISIT MOLLY JEND'S SPACE SERVER ONGOING PRIVATE PARTY?

Molly Jend, now there's a name that used to be synonymous with Willem Floures. She was always a good friend until we had a falling out of sorts. I said some things, she said some things and we kind of never apologized. But that place, "Space Server," is this exclusive VIP party central that never dies. The music can be heard for miles (not really, that just sounds cooler than saying "music is really loud") and she has successfully turned the house into a business and the business into a success.

People pay in hourly blocks to be a part of the exclusivity.

Yeah…

You could say Jend and I were an item.

The idea for Space Server, more or less, began as a joke during those few summer months when we were the opposite of productivity, wasting every day and night on leisure spillover and sinful commodities.

Producer voice speaks to me instead of speaking to 'X' but clearly what I hear is not meant for my ears.

"I didn't tell him to smear the chat. Have you heard anything about Sugar smearing this broadcast?!"

Smearing as in crashing, as in intentionally going against the script.

I don't know what's wrong.

Producer voice says what I don't want to hear:

## WHAT THE HELL ARE YOU TALKING ABOUT?

My reply should be:

## I AM TALKING ABOUT MYSELF
## WHO ELSE?

What if I'm not?

The point is I'm talking.

I am being honest. I mean, right? I didn't do this to smear the show. I actually enjoy these chats. The audience actually has a voice, even if it's italicized and withheld until the end of the broadcast.

If you ask me a question, I can't help but answer honestly.

Producer voice goes back to the script I believed I had been following:

## WHAT PART OF YOU DIED ON DECEMBER 3RD?

Sensitive question but this is a "tell-all" kind of event.

I find it effortless to type out my reply rather than form it in mouth, tone, hanging there, the sound of my voice, which always sounds uncertain, unconfident of what I might say.

December 3rd was a day I had forgotten.

It was a day when part of me died.

Guess we want to go there.

Do we really want to go there?

I imagine X has already answered. I picture his response to be long paragraphs with proper punctuation. My lines are jagged, cut and trim. It's because I could never type fast enough. Computer literate I am not.

Never mind, though, because I get the point across.

What happened, how it involved the slicing of wrists, the depression of a top ten fighter. He succumbed to those thoughts, our thoughts, the thoughts that don't make any sense until they circle around like a shark on bad days when every cut, every strike, is augmented twice as large, twice as deadly.

I hurt most on those days.

Random seizures of bad memories.

He was young and hadn't survived very many of these shame spirals.

A week after we fought he lost a second time.

The escaping into long drawn out lacerations up the forearm. I thought about that, seeing and imagining what it must feel like to cut and watch as the blade goes in deep.

I hear that the pain is slower than the bloodletting.

Blood surges out of those cuts but the pain, the kind of pain that's lasting, waits patiently until the realization hits:

You've done it.

You have no way of undoing what has been done.

Yeah...

On December 3rd, Willem "Lucky Strike" Floures committed suicide.

It felt like I lost a part of me when really I had won.

## CANDID

They want candid but they want the truth.

Producer voice doesn't accept my words, the truth, again with the worry that I'm going against the script.

Hey now, I'm answering every question.

When the producer says, "You're getting them all wrong!" and, "Are you forgetting yourself?" it begins to sink in. Shame.

Same feeling.

Same uncertain response:

## I THINK SO

Spencer is pissed.

He must be. Somehow I'm not. It's like I'm watching from the sidelines as I destroy my entire career. What must this look like, an old fighter acting all senile, forgetting the facts, fibbing and falling into some kind of fiction he truly believed to be the truth?

Shit.

And X must be doing well.

Producer voice with another prompt:

## YOU FOUGHT WITH A BROKEN HAND ONCE. TELL US ABOUT IT. SPECIFICALLY, HOW YOU AVOIDED LOSING DESPITE SUCH A DEBILITATING INJURY

I believe I broke my right hand when I landed a punch to 'The Assassin's' skull. He ducked and as he did, my power punch hit the top of his head rather than flush on his nose and forehead.

Hear that snap. I was sure that it was bone breaking, the sound is unmistakable, but I hadn't realized that it was the ligaments in my hand that caved. With a few light jabs, it became all too real that something was up.

Note: If you are ever in a situation where you break your hand, do not advertise the fact that you have broken your hand by holding it up high, gripping to a shout of anguish and pain.

You do that and you better believe there will be more pain.

Punches thrown.

The fight continued. I couldn't tell myself to stop. Who really has that kind of control?

The Assassin wanted to win just like I wanted to win.

In the end I won with a broken hand, relying on left hooks and power shots, jabbing through the pain if only so that I demonstrated how I could fight through that pain. It wasn't going to work against me.

Post-fight conferences highlighted how I had broken my hand.

The positivity that came from the reaction to something so unfortunate was a textbook example of the irony of being memorable and relevant in this society. You had to hurt yourself in order to be heard. You have to continue working, being productive, doing whatever it is that you do to maintain their attention. If no one pays attention to you, you aren't really alive.

The desperation of the cure.

Some want infamy. Some want fame.

Some fight. Some love. Some follow rather than lead.

Everybody wants to be remembered.

The fight will be remembered not for such a triumphant win but because I broke my hand. Never mind how I fought through the pain.

Never mind how I fought one of my best fights.

Just stay with the negligible fact that my right jab will never again be the same. Once you break your hand, it never heals fully, not when you are fighting the way I am fighting.

That became the big concern:

Question on people's minds: How much of a hindrance exactly?

## WHY THE REMATCH? WHY NOW? GIVEN REPORTS THAT YOU CLAIM IT IS TIME TO RETIRE, WHY BOTHER TO REPEAT THE LOSS?

Assuming I lose. What's the point in pretending that the odds are not stacked against me? They are.

Producer voice in my ear warning me—

## STICK TO THE SCRIPT

I do just that but seemingly nothing changes.

Producer is still upset.

Can't make everyone happy.

X takes the question and I assume he types out a wondrous explanation because I am not asked to reply.

I hold back, watching as they ignore my would-be reply.

## WHAT IS BETTER—EIGHT, TWELVE, OR FIFTEEN ROUNDS?

X would go with twelve, I'm sure of it.

I have fought a few fifteen rounder fights during my career and let me tell you, when you know that you have that many ahead of you, the fight becomes more conservative. I don't throw as many flurries; I play more defensively.

Either you get an early knockout or you are basically there for the decision. You watch one of my fights and you know that it'll likely go to decision. Not a problem but yes it's still a problem because the audience wants the SHOCK and AWE of a KO.

They want that so much more than seeing the sweet science in effect.

X probably mentions something about how he has the conditioning to last a twenty round fight if there was such a thing.

I assume that he's very smug about it.

Treats this prompt with a lack of care.

I would have done the same at that age.

I did. Something about facing yourself in the ring that changes the way you treat yourself outside of the fight. You see yourself from a distance like you see yourself throwing fists and aiming for your loss.

I feel distant even now, especially now, as I watch these words form in perfect type. I assume the audience isn't pleased with my performance.

These words are mine.

Are they really?

## CANDID

There's that problem then, the fact that I'm getting this wrong, getting it all wrong. How can you change anything if you don't see why you are wrong? And these memories of mine, they are as real as anything can be...I know they are right, facts from 'Sugar' Willem Floures's past...but producer voice denies the facts, providing evidence revealing that I'm full of shit.

How is that?

I lived through these events; I was there.

Seems I'm full of questions.

## THE LAUGHTER

We continue like this for quite some time.

I get prompts and I fail to answer them correctly, with the script in mind; like I said, I can't fix what I can't identify to be the problem. They tell me that I am forgetting myself and I fear that it might be true.

That might be the case.

I've got how many fights left in me…?

Two?

And I'm barely in the spotlight anymore.

Executioner, 'X,' the prodigy, the man that carries our name well, Willem Floures, looks to be everything I used to be.

What frightens me the most is what is laced in laughter:

## WHAT IF HE IS BETTER?

What if he makes better decisions, fights more strategically, builds a better defense, and simply makes better sense of his life?

What does that mean for me?

I am overshadowed, poor version of an identity that I held for a time.

I hear the laughter but it makes me happy.

The laughter most dear is the laughter that I heard from the audience when I used to be hilarious. They used to laugh at my jokes.

Now they just laugh at me.

## CANDID

Producer voice asks for a follow-up. Something I can say off-the-cuff.

So I say something about the fight and how I am confident that my strategy going into the fight will overwrite any of the error seen in the original fight—this includes my excessive clinching, holding, and fighting on the defensive for over half of the fight.

Playing off the retirement rumor, my fault, I explain how I want to go out with a bang, a big ONE, TWO, THREE, trio of wins.

I intend going out with a win rather than a whimper.

Not what the producer wants, and I know that, but it's okay because I am telling the truth. I know that I'm telling the truth.

I can only say what I know to be true.

And if they are lies, there is something far worse, completely beyond my control, at work here. I can (and will) worry about what I am not and what I used to be but I cannot stomach what it means to be a blemish, nothing but a sequence of crisis and collapse.

How much more declarative must I be?

## WILDCARD

The prompt about physical training.

Withhold the fact that I haven't started yet and won't be for weeks (what a waste); instead, I talk about how embracing the unexpected is about as good a strategy as any. Executioner expects what I expect; he expects that I will work on trying to surprise him. The trick then is to focus on predicting the surprise and proving to layer surprise on the surprise.

A mouthful, potentially impossible, but what else do they want to hear?

Producer voice in my ear asks:

## WHAT DO YOU MEAN?
## YOU ARE NOT MAKING SENSE

I don't make sense.
As a fighter.
As a person.
I don't make sense.
Is that the official word?
Or the word on the street?

## IS ANYONE LAUGHING?

According to everyone, this is all incorrect. Does not fit with recorded history. So, then, if it isn't true then this entire episode, this entire event, consists of lies. Seems I'm living a lie that I can't live down.

What the hell does that mean?

I mean really…

I only know what I know, and if it happens to be wrong, a lie, then okay:

I am living a lie.

## I GUESS THAT'S WHY I BECAME A FIGHTER

Everything that doesn't make sense, I beat the shit out of me until it does.

Even if it doesn't, the right punch will shake free the worry, the worry that's all about how I'm nearing middle-age and I'm nowhere closer to coming to grips with who I am than when I was just starting out, burning cigarettes onto my skin just to feel something, getting into fights in front of bars in hopes of getting the chance to steal someone's wallet.

Basically being the rebel, what I thought I should be.

Should have been.

Seemed to embody.

But no.

I was basically just lost, trying way too many paths while never actually committing to one.

Or, put more simply:

I am a fighter.

I am incapable of loving others including myself.

## WHO ARE YOU BUT STRANGERS IN A CROWD?

Later, after I hear from Spencer and I hear from the world various comments and hurtful comments like:

## HE'S SENILE

## HE'S OUT OF HIS MIND.

## HE'S ON DRUGS.

## HE'S A WRECK.

Many of those from Spencer himself, I am solemn, quiet,

enjoying nothing while trying my best to merge into the nothingness of the hotel room where we will stay the night, each in our own bed, not talking to each other, not talking about the incoming fight, not talking about the big problem, which has everything to do with an escaped identity.

Not talking.

Not helping.

No help at all.

Willem Floures, do you know of the man, the myth, the fighter?

I thought I did but I guess not.

## CANDID

I will ask only once during the night, in the dark, lightless room, when I know that Spencer is not asleep, but has his eyes closed, trying his best to pretend that he is at rest, complete with fake snoring:

"What about training?"

He will pretend to ignore me, but the fact that I asked will bother him.

Spencer will have to answer.

And he'll say what he always says:

"We'll get to that."

We always do, but by the time we hit the heavy bag, the ten-to-twenty mile run, the training routine in full, the fight can be seen, looming in the distance of next week. I'll ask Spencer, "Why didn't we train? Why didn't we focus on a longer, more effective regimen?"

His response is the response of a trainer, an agent, a longtime friend that has lost confidence in his project, lost confidence in me:

## CANDID

"The truth is that no amount of improvement to your body will make any difference. If you are going to win, you need to win using fight psychology."

According to the only "friend" I have, I have a slim to nil chance of winning and even if I did, it would be less on skill and more to do with luck.

I'll admit that this isn't very reassuring at all.

It kind of makes me feel like a nuisance.

Makes me worry about what the world really thinks and what they will think about 'Sugar' in the weeks and years after my inevitable demise, my retirement from the sport.

Makes me think about how I can prove them all wrong.

All of them.

Spencer, yes, you too.

I get to thinking...

## A THOUGHT

And it comes to me on that same night, dark room, the orchestration of slumber without any real truth.

And it takes me a week or two of media junkets to fathom what I need to do to begin.

And it takes a single sentence to turn the attention around onto me, limelight and thrill.

And it's a sentence from a different kind of story:

## I KILLED A MAN

And it doesn't fit.

And that's why it would work.

Why it would turn the fight around and maybe, just maybe, I'd have a chance to win. Like Spencer said—

Only real chance I have is to psych X out.

Yeah well, how's this for psyching someone out?

# VERSUS

A hurtful but hopeful thing to say:

## THIS IS WHAT YOU DID WRONG

I'm supposed to learn from my mistakes.

I learn from the mistakes but I lose it all during the lecture. Spencer sits me down in a seat like this is Sunday school and draws on a dry-erase board to the constant playback of the fight.

*The* fight.

Executioner at his prime, Sugar losing favor.

Spencer isn't about to analyze what I looked like, or even how hard I worked leading up to the fight. No, he zeroes in on the omission.

Punches not thrown.

Punches not blocked.

This is what I did wrong, and I might have won the match but Spencer would still sit me down for an hour-long lecture. Clean KO or biggest loss, Spencer will still preach; he will show me where I went wrong.

"To start with, how many times have I said to land first attack?"

First attack meaning first jab, first impact—

Like it's some kind of competition.

Wait a minute...

When isn't it a form of competition?

When are we not fighting to better understand ourselves?

"I agree," my go-to reply during post-fight analysis lecture holy-shit-how-long-is-this-going-to-take-please-blow-my-brains-out come on I understand, I understand. How is this helping?

We're wasting time.
I should be training.

## ROUND ONE

X hops forward, two-stepping around the ring taunting me.
I put my fists up.

## SHELL

I play it defensively.
I do not land the first punch.
First punch is a jab.

## JAB

X leads jab, jab, jab, jab, all of them absorbed. They aren't landing clean, but tell that to the audience, the CompuBox fuckers, the crooked judges that want me out of the picture. This league needs the new and improved. I do a poor representation of myself. They want a Willem that reminds them not of the times but of the timeless. They want my prime performance.

They want to forget that we are all aging, squirming in our shells.

Try and forget that as you age so too does your personality.

You are not the same person you were when you walked into this fight.

This is what they really want.

I land my first.

## JAB

Round one starts slow, feeling out X, waiting for his strategy to present itself. I know it can only be one of four possible plans. When I was his age, I didn't have a whole lot of patience. I had to outbox everyone.

Spencer scowls, "What is this passive bullshit?"

And:
"That's not you!"
Actually, it is.
Who else would I be?

## JAB
## ATTEMPTED HOOK TO THE BODY

Not my best. I lead with the right not quite sure of what I'm thinking. It's because X had me down for the ten count long before this fight. I had psyched myself out of the dance long before sole met canvas.

Spencer cups his hands, "My god, why didn't you block any of those jabs?"

## JAB
## JAB
## JAB
## JAB
## STRAIGHT TO THE CHIN

I didn't see them coming.
But don't tell him that.
"I was buying an opportunity."
My excuse.
Spencer rubs his eyes, "You can't afford to do that any more, you understand?"
Again, this time louder, writing on the dry-erase board:

## CONSERVATIVE
## BOXER-PUNCHER

"This is what you need to be!"
He circles it once, twice...four, five times.
"This is what you need to be!"
Louder this time.
Back to the fight.
Round two is about to start.

## ROUND TWO

As he said, round two is where I got it all wrong and I'll admit that it's true.

"My fucking god, what the hell were you thinking?!"

Spencer is starting to sweat. I played right into X's plan and what hurts the most is that I came up with this tactic. It's mine, all mine, and yet he uses it and worst of all, I let it happen. I fell into line and blocked the jabs.

## BLOCK
## SUDDEN IMPACT

Problem is the jabs were ploys for the cutting shot right to the body.

He lands three well-formed punches, all of them straight shots, to the body where I hadn't been prepared to take a three-punch flurry.

I narrowly block the uppercut X continued to use throughout the fight. The uppercut that would eventually end the fight in round eight, sending me to the ground where for a brief moment I lost sight of where I was and all I wanted to do was sleep. Take a nap. The ring might as well have been a queen-sized bed.

I was out cold.

But round two, I was a little more active.

JAB
JAB
STRAIGHT
JAB
STRAIGHT
JAB
JAB
STRAIGHT
BLOCK
DUCK
TO THE BODY

JAB
JAB
HOLD

"Why are you holding?"

Spencer widens his eyes, "Explain that to me because I'm dumbfounded."

"Explain why…"

"Why would you hold? You should have used the goddamn left hook!"

I watch the footage. I avoid scrutiny with a yawn.

"If you weren't that lax in the ring, you might have won this!"

Another combination, attempted, alongside with notice of which punches actually landed:

JAB (miss)
JAB (miss)
HOOK TO BODY (miss)
HOOK TO THE FACE (miss)
BACKPEDAL (to avoid X's own jab)
BLOCK (wait for it)
JAB OUT OF POSITION (fight out of it)
JAB (miss)
JAB (impact)
STRAIGHT TO FACE (impact)

I tell Spencer, "That wasn't so bad, right?"

He watches, silent for a moment, as X follows it up with a combination that turns into the first flurry that stuns me. I am able to fight out of it, holding once or twice, not that anyone noticed.

Spencer sighs.

Except for Spencer.

"It's bad."

Solemnly, he returns to the dry-erase board and writes down a phrase to be further explored later, "Footwork & energy management."

I think my footwork is fine.

Not that I say anything.
Round three is about to start.

## ROUND THREE

I do better this round but what the audience doesn't realize is that it's not because I stunned X or even managed to hurt him.

It's because he took the round off. I should have identified that he was merely resting, saving it up (much to his dismay, because I know how little patience I have for that kind of thing) in order to send me down to the canvas in round four, five, and for good in round eight.

Spencer writes on the dry-erase board, "Round management."

Management.

He might as well just write that on the board and save some time.

Manage this old, confused fighter. Help me figure out why the moment I step into the ring, I feel gassed, completely absent, detached from my body.

Seeing this should make me feel better. I land a classic combination, not that it does anything to X. He takes it in stride, trading shots with me until I reach out and clinch, because truth is I'm winded, I'm hurt, I'm tired, and most of all, I'm confused.

The combination:

JAB
JAB
NOTICE AN OPENING TO THE BODY
JAB TO BODY
HOOK TO LEFT SIDE OF FACE
HOOK TO BODY
STRAIGHT
STRAIGHT
JAB
SHORT CROSS TO THE BODY
LEFT POWER SHOT (MY BEST)

I give him my best combination, finishing it off with a

clean power shot to the body, something that should have at least registered but X, as I had said earlier, follows up with a combination of his own.

I shut my eyes, not wanting to see it.

I hear Spencer breathing heavily, "Unacceptable! You are falling into your own traps!"

I am.

Yes.

I know that I am.

How can I avoid the past's snares and spikes if I forget where I had left them, and moreover, what can you do if every time I look in the mirror I see someone new, someone older, someone that I'm not at all familiar with?

This is me, I say.

But I don't believe it.

## ROUND FOUR

X uses this round to catch up on the cards.

The round is a mess. I am stunned early and I hold.

Much of round four looks like this:

BLOCK
X LANDS A COMBINATION
COMBINATION CONSISTS OF:
JAB
LEFT HOOK
JAB
LEFT HOOK
RIGHT HOOK
JAB
STRAIGHT
TO THE BODY:
JAB
JAB
POWER SHOT STRAIGHT
POWER SHOT STRAIGHT
UPPERCUT (impact, stun)

My best bet is, of course:

BLOCK
HOLD
BLOCK
BRACE FOR IMPACT
HOLD
BLOCK
HOLD

Spencer's head is in his hands, not even watching.

I can hear him say, "You don't need me to tell you. I'm sure you're still feeling the impact of that left hook."

I tell him that I am.

The left hook heard around the world.

"That should have been your left hook."

It used to be mine.

Now all I do is hold.

HOLD
HOLD
HOLD
HOLD

Even though he doesn't knock me down, the judges score round four an "eight," two points that hit right at the heart. The round goes to Executioner.

It's because I performed little more than the role of the punching bag.

I took the punches and grabbed for dear life.

X mumbled about thirty seconds from the end of the round:

*What is wrong with you?*

You tell me.

I'm kind of finding it difficult to say much of anything.

## ROUND FIVE

*No comment.*

That's the official statement.

Spencer stares at the dry-erase board, baffled at the scribble.

"You need a lot of work…"

You can say that again.

He stuns me this round with something that doesn't quite register but it definitely stung. Much like a bee sting, it tingled and then shot right to the back of my brain, a numbing pain.

It's the uppercut.

The same damn uppercut.

I was always good at carefully throwing in an uppercut at the end of a combination. I could really get the glove right under the chin, the kind of punch that sends glassjaws crying and cast-iron chins to the ground.

Not that I ever really did.

During my prime, I fought more just like me.

We took the punches like we planned on early retirement. They wear on you over the years. I wonder how bad my memory, my reflexes, my conditioning will be five, ten, fifteen years from now.

But okay, the uppercut.

Didn't see it coming (which means X did a great job connecting).

I don't remember how long I was on the ground but it wasn't for long. You fight enough and you can get by for a while, at least half the fight, on instinct, muscle memory, the routine of having heard, smelled, and felt pretty much everything you'd expect in a fight.

Sensory cues from decades of self-affliction.

Remnants of a fighter that can't stop fighting himself.

## ROUND SIX

It all comes apart after that uppercut knockdown in the fifth.

Spencer is silent, chews gum. Watches in silent dismay.

It's bad, and he's no longer bothering to rant or even comment.

I get the sense that he wants to shut the footage off as much as I do; however, it stays on as I look like a wreck in round six.

X has me pinned against the ropes for a third of the round.

## BLOCK
## HOLD
## SHORT LIFELESS HOOKS TO THE BODY

It's what I do to survive.

To the referee it appeared as though I was all right.

Can't say that I was but again, fighter's instinct.

"Were there any lights on during the last three rounds?"

Can't say that there were so I don't say anything.

Spencer blows a bubble, lets it pop and hang over his lower lip for a few seconds before pulling it back into his mouth with his tongue.

"Rookie mistake."

## ROUND SEVEN

So by now everyone in the audience expects X to win. If it goes to decision, X is victor, no doubt about it. This is one of those cases where I basically have to knock him out in order to win.

And that wasn't going to happen.

Everyone knew it.

People stood up and left.

There were a few rounds left in the fight but it seemed as though everyone had it all fought out in their mind. They knew how it would end. We fought it out, lagging behind the times.

I watch the footage, not at all familiar with what happened in round seven.

I was out on my feet, nothing there.

You know how everything is muted when underwater, both sight and sound cloudy and obtuse?

That's how it feels after being stunned, your mind slush, random thoughts, sometimes as odd as the last time you called your mom, rise up from the grey matter of your memory.

For me, round seven was all about hamburgers. I tasted a bacon cheeseburger, craved it, after the half-memory of eating a double-decker at a local restaurant resurfaced somewhere towards the beginning of the round.

I could go for one right about now...

Spencer runs his palm across the dry-erase board, smearing everything he'd written. Conceivably, this would be alarming. *Conceivably.*

Yeah, well I'm just hopeful that there won't be a follow-up lecture.

I mean look at what I'm doing:

> JAB
> JAB
> JAB
> JAB
> HOLD

Versus what X is doing:

> BLOCK
> WEEVE-JAB TO BODY
> LEFT HOOK
> RIGHT HOOK
> STRAIGHT

Keep in mind that this is all news to me.

Can't recall what happened this round.

Turns out I didn't miss anything. I missed every single punch thrown, leaving myself open fifty percent of the time for X to throw in a combination, score more points, make me look terrible.

It's a horrible performance. I admit it.

When I attempt to clinch, I leave myself wide open. X sees every single clinch coming so what does he do?

> BACK PEDAL
> TWO STEPS

## LEAN BACK
## WATCH ME GRAB AIR
## PERFECT STRAIGHT
## HOOK TO THE FACE

I don't cut easily. I have taken a lot of damage these last couple decades, compounded misery on layaway, but hell if I've kept myself fairly clean, give or take a welt or two on occasion.

But blood flows by round seven from the wound on my face that would swell and become the welt that led me to the hospital.

Take one of those dry-erase markers and draw a face on the welt and from a far enough distance, from the POV of a druggie or drunk son-of-a-bitch, they just might figure the welt for a conjoined twin, a second face, skull and all. It swelled and throbbed and pained me for hours, a day, even now I feel numb to the touch on that side of my face.

The painkillers, you see.

Spencer sighs.

Says nothing.

Here it comes.

## ROUND EIGHT

Wow, the welt is already forming; the referee pulls me aside and says something to me. Can't hear it from the side of the ring but it's the usual measure of consciousness. Answer the question:

Is this fighter out on his feet or is he still fighting?

The referee should have called it right then and there. Part of me is glad that he didn't because it's far more embarrassing to lose the fight between rounds; however, what happened next, about a minute into round eight, might have been one of the worst experiences of my life.

You'll see what I mean.

I still see the sequence in slow motion.

X opts to let me try for the clinch but for a time, about fifteen seconds, we are at a standstill, waiting.

He waits for another stupid mistake.

I'm waiting to fall asleep. The audience wants this to be over and those that remain in their seats are only there in hopes of seeing a KO.

## JAB

He toys around with the jab.

## JAB

I block one but absorb the next.

## JAB

He wants me to fight.
X knows that he has the fight won; he's looking for the perfect time to plant that exclamation point on VICTORY.

## JAB

He gets there quickly, with the single most important tool in the sweet science that is boxing.

## JAB

I block.

## JAB

Again, I block.

## JAB

Only a matter of time and the time is now.
I absorb the jab and try for my own. Grazes his glove, which he then uses as an opportunity to threaten me with an outlandish, taunting haymaker.
I narrowly block it.
He grins, mouthpiece showing, 'XXX' can be seen printed

across the piece. The audience is a low roar, everyone sensing blood.

JAB
JAB
JAB

Trio of jabs, two hitting me right on the nose, shaking me free, doing the trick by sending a signal, ANGER, from some part of my mind that's still somehow working and you know what happens next. What happens next is exactly what X wanted to happen.

I foolishly go for the clinch.

I grab air.

## NOTHING

And something for any highlight reel:

Perfectly executed uppercut, landing right under the chin.

And I fall back, perhaps because I was still grabbing for him I end up grabbing the ropes on my way down. I bounce back upon reaching for the top rope, stumbling in two directions, one of them happens to be X.

As if coming back for more, he hits me again.

## UPPERCUT

And I hear laughter.

I look like a ragdoll being tossed around.

To the ground I go and Spencer stops the footage.

I fill in the rest.

Their laughter.

Laughing at me.

For a moment, the way the video is paused, each of my arms going a different direction from my legs, which are floating, on my face the expression of sinister confusion: I feel the tickle of a giggle rising from the base of my throat. I burst out into laughter.

Spencer says, "You think this shit is funny?"

Fact of the matter is, I don't.
I find it all frightening.
I will never sleep well again.
At night I hear that laughter, the lacerating kind that feels like another fight in and of itself, twelve rounds of ridicule, the roast of 'Sugar' Willem Floures by all the others that know more about him than he knows himself.
The receiving end of all jokes.
It's as bad as an inside joke that I'm not in on...
And it's about me.

## WHAT NOW?
## SILENCE

I stop laughing and I'm only a cough away from crying.
Spencer sighs, he rewinds the footage and replays the KO again.

## THAT PERFECT UPPERCUT
## THE UPPERCUT HEARD AROUND THE WORLD

Are they satisfied?
Spencer makes a face, "It is you when you were twenty-two."
Shakes his head, "Right down to the penchant for combinations."
He shuts off the footage, looks at the dry-erase board.

## SILENCE

Everything he had written is now a smear.
"'Sugar'...you are no longer sweet with the science."
I feel the side of my face. This would be sore if I were sober.
He turns to me, "Well?"
I raise my eyebrows, "Well what?"
"Got any bright ideas?"

## SILENCE

But I only hear laughter.

We sit here for a time, drifting between caustic thoughts and, at least for me, a deepening fear that is borderline indescribable.

I say, "You shouldn't have signed us up for the rematch."

Spencer sighs, "We have no choice. You take the rematch or you no longer exist. 'Fade out on a sorry sack of shit.' You want that? Because I don't. I've spent the last three decades building you into the definition of Willem Floures. 'Sugar' as in sweet; 'sweet' as in the sweetest display of the science that is boxing. And look at you now…"

## SILENCE

I have nothing to say.

Thankfully, I am not left with the laughter for long, the laughter exclusively for me. Spencer still speaks for me, and what he says next is about as succinct and on-point as anything I could have hoped to hear:

*You either win or you wither away.*

This is it. In terms of chances, I'm on my last and I'm lucky to have one more. Very discouraging when you look in the mirror, you look at any form of identification, and you are no clearer in your comprehension of what it means to be THIS person than you were ten, twenty, thirty years ago.

Follow that up by something a trainer and agent should never ask their client, their fighter, their friend:

"Got any ideas? Because I'm done."

As a matter of fact, I do.

Remember what I had said earlier, about that little flicker that became something full-featured and, at least during this era of desperation, became a fantastic idea? Yeah well when Spencer Mullen seems to get behind it and approve of such an idea, what would you do?

You go along with it.

You even get a little excited.

Maybe, just maybe, you think that you might have a chance.

# I MIGHT WIN

Old age does not bring wisdom.
Old age turns smart minds into fools.

# THE SILENCE I SEEK

A lot of what I don't like might follow me wherever I go, but there is one place that saves me from the shame, the swarming of scrutiny and shit talking. It really doesn't look like much, older two story house just outside the city, slightly neglected lawn, paint job on the place faded, in need of a facelift.

It is a lived-in home.

Spencer's house since as far back as his previous life. It is also where I reside when I'm not on the road, on a plane, shoved into another stunt, or stunned by an uppercut in the eighth round of a fight that I'd rather forget.

The house looks a lot like me.

It creaks with every step just like my knees make a snapping sound as I sit down. This house isn't much at all, but maybe neither am I.

I like it here.

It feels like I can push everything, the pressure, away; it's almost like I can leave it all outside.

The world does not pass the front door.

Here, there is silence.

Here, this is where I escape.

Where I live, that apartment somewhere posing as my place, broken into more than a handful of times by desperate media seeking something of me, might as well not even exist. I might as well just consider the world out there as unreachable.

Because when I retreat to the calm of the house, it feels like I no longer exist. And you know what?

I like the fact that I can lose it all with a single step into the house.

It swallows us whole and it feels like we operate on an entirely different spectrum of time. Spencer was always aware of this fact.

I'm not the only one that finds worth in the home. He offered me one of the spare rooms, "Fuck if I think you'll get any solace anywhere else."

The house holds onto a simpler time.

That's what I believe, anyway. Spencer would never tell you but he never got over the passing of his wife. It happened quickly, the details omitted, but the fact that he drove away the grief by fixating on something all-encompassing as boxing, he began a new era of his life.

The previous era, I imagine, is felt in the confines of this home.

His daughter, Sarah, nine years of age, has the house and it's hauntings to take care of her whenever Spencer leaves for work.

No nannies, no daycare—

Spencer can leave and Sarah never feels like she's been left alone.

There's something about the house…

And hear that?

## SILENCE

It is what I seek. Especially now, given what we must do.

So I have to admit that I can't believe that Spencer thinks it's a good idea. A good idea…admitting to murder. A good idea… sensationalizing and lying about fiction made fact. A good idea… no-showing all of today's prefight media events. A good idea…

How much is it worth?

Is it really worth the calm, the silence that helps settle those bothersome thoughts?

## SILENCE

Sarah skips into the kitchen, sits with us at the table, listens to talk about theoretical murder made 'true.'

Sarah giggles, "Are you going to die?"

"Maybe," Spencer grins, "maybe."

I tell him about how it might not catch on. I tell him, "Really how easy is it to pretend you murdered someone?"

Spencer's reply: "Easier than you'd believe."
"What about name, motive, all of that?"

## YOU CAN LIE ABOUT THAT

"Why don't you go back upstairs and play?"
Sarah frowns, "But James won't let me back into my room."
James. Just another one of those hauntings, I gather. The names change every time; as far as I'm concerned, I haven't come across any of those so-called hauntings. Neither has Spencer. Product of a child's imagination? Well, there *is* something here, something about the house, but I'm not about to try to explain it. I like it here. Isn't that enough?
"Well tell James to play nice."
Sarah skips around the kitchen table.
She punches me in the arm, "I punched you."
Pained expression, "Yes you did."
"Did it hurt?"
Actually it did. She got me right where I was already sore.
Turning to Spencer, "Your daughter knows how to throw a punch."
"Course she does. Her father is Spencer Mullen."
Sarah shadowboxes, "I fought James once. I won!"
"Good girl," Spencer sips cold coffee from a mug.
We've been sitting here, scheming, not getting anywhere. Doubt on my end, assurance on his, we mostly drink coffee while scouring the internet on our respective laptops, attempting to find something to use.
Material, an image, I don't know.
Ask Spencer and he tells me:

## YOU CAN LIE ABOUT THAT

"Lie about what?"
Say anything. It can be true if they believe it to be true.
Sarah runs up the stairs, leaving Spencer and I to the unproductivity of this day. Waste of a day. Spencer is determined that this will help rebuild some of the cache I have lost.

"You know we were supposed to continue with prefight promotions," I warn Spencer, given that he's usually the one stressing out about this kind of stuff.

Spencer types something, looks up at me, screen glow causing him to appear pale, malnourished, "I have something in mind."

When I ask, he shakes his head, "Later."

Later becomes much later becomes a lot of wasting time searching websites, playing free browser videogames while Spencer types away at something he won't show me until "later."

## LATER

After the painkillers start to wear off and I sit still, not moving at all, staring at my screensaver—a series of colorful psychedelic light shows—because to move an inch is to send radiating waves of pain up my arm, my leg, across my face.

I sit still because pain has me pinned.

"Okay," Spencer says, sigh of relief.

## WHAT IS IT?

Well, it's a bunch of lies.

If it doesn't make any sense, lie until it does.

Okay, I'll do my best to summarize:

## HE HAS A PAST

As in, I have a past history of violence.

As in, I have been known to partake in drunken misconduct.

As in, there have been a lot of bar fights.

As in, pretty much anyone would agree, given that I'm a fighter and that bar fights are so common someone will step up and attest to the lie, validating it via testimony.

As in, whatever we don't have an answer to, we'll lie about it later.

As in, I might have taken a knife to a man during one of these quarrels.

As in, I should have been training but instead I was busy

blacking out during the killing.

As in, that's my cover story:

My excuse for not remembering.

As in, I will plead innocent and in pleading innocent, people will think I'm even guiltier than they thought.

As in, there is a missing dead man, no longer in this world, dead by my drunken hands.

As in, it's all a lie but the search for evidence will fuel promotions, sending the media my way.

As in, all news is good news, no matter if it's terrible, bad, slanderous.

As in, you will know me in the next couple days as "that boxer guy who killed a man."

As in, the world is fickle, but the media-outlets are far worse.

## A TERRIBLE PAST

I have my reservations about all of it but it was my idea, remember?

Can't back down now.

I move into the other room, leaving my laptop and that link to anxiety, on the kitchen table. Spencer follows me, carrying the laptop, reading aloud a dizzying list of deceit.

## YOU CAN LIE ABOUT THAT

"If you haven't a clue, it doesn't matter 'cause you killed a man and everyone will believe it even if they don't."

Where is my heart?

Why is my heart not in this?

I can lie to Spencer, you know. I can lie, saying that I'm excited, that this will be a boon for us. However, what I think about as I sit down on the old couch, the couch that always smells of chocolate ever since Sarah accidentally spilled hot chocolate into the cushions. No amount of cleaning washes away the smell. Frankly, I look forward to it. It pulls me out of my head and back into the house, this room, right now.

Here I am.

I want to relax.

The pain numbs the soul.

I look like I'm listening.

I look and act like I am tuned into our "most deadly" little plan.

I look the part but really there's only one thing I'm listening to:

## SILENCE

The silence I seek is right here, cradling my beat-the-shit-up body, carrying me away, in search of one of those hauntings.

I seek an adventure, if only because by going on an adventure, I will be going somewhere else. Somewhere away from Willem. Meaning, I want to step outside myself. I am often way too self-absorbed and not because I care so much about this identity but because I feel obligated.

I am not the only Willem Floures.

There are forty-one of us. A whole league.

I am number two, which means I'm not number one. How can you be second best to yourself? Does it make any sense to you because it doesn't to me. The internal monologue isn't mine. I hear voices, all of their would-be voices, discussing dreams, ambitions, and what it means to be 'me.'

Sometimes I just want to be a person.

Not this personality.

The pressure to keep fighting is the force of the fight itself; we fight to entertain and to be enlightened. I am not so sure I've achieved any sort of enlightenment. Once, back when I was minted as "undefeated" and destined to build and brand the league as one of the best, the premier boxing syndication worldwide, I thought I knew.

I thought I saw it, that spark in my eyes.

"It's me," that's what I said.

In the mirror, I see the shadow take shape.

My silhouette is cookie-cutter, just another permutation of the identity that is 'Willem Floures.'

We all manage to look, act, speak, and spell the same.

That seems remarkable until ~~you~~ realize—
Scratch that—until I realize what's at work here.
Don't ask.
If you do, guess what?

## YOU CAN LIE ABOUT THAT

I will be forced into another lie.

Never was very comfortable, barely any good at, lying but when you have an agent like Spencer who does all the talking for you, I just have to be there. Just barely.

Funny then, to come to another realization (it must be the fact that I am just so comfortable, most at ease, when in this house):

I am a fighter that has always loathed the act of fighting.

The sweet science is one of the most difficult to master and somewhere I found out that I was a natural. Well…maybe the truth is:

## YOU CAN LIE ABOUT THAT TOO

I proclaimed myself a fighter and not just a fighter but a:

## STRATEGIST

Not a boxer-puncher, not a brawler, not a throwback kind of style. I defined 'Willem Floures's to be a strategist. Meaning: I am all of the above. Meaning: I am full of shit. We are all full of shit. I mean, come on, a fight is a lot like a dance: it takes two to get things going.

Swing and a miss.

Round by round edge-of-your-seat fighting isn't possible if I am not who I think I am. See how I am a contradiction?

Which part of me will inevitably change/fix that problem.

I used to think it was me; I'd be the one to make things work.

## SILENCE

So the murder, the lies, will be enough to buoy an entire campaign Spencer has conceived tonight, as of this evening, four hours of what I had felt to be unproductive surfing the net. Guess I was the one wasting time, not Spencer. He also talks about how X will become a nonissue, might even be psyched out by the idea of having murdered someone.

What I wonder is:

"If I claimed to have killed someone, wouldn't that mean X killed someone too?"

"No," Spencer replies, "but yes. But no." Never looks up from the screen.

## YOU CAN LIE ABOUT THAT

"If you need to," Spencer adds.

I killed a man.

It still feels strange to say these words.

I haven't actually said them aloud.

Spencer says that I should.

That I have to.

"Say it, I want to hear you say it. You need to get used to saying it."

Close one eye, open the other. Fine—

## I KILLED A MAN

The statement hangs there, like I just carved through a curtain of space, rendering it wounded, broken, a black hole.

"You sound like you don't mean it."

True. True statement. I don't mean it.

I don't want to mean it.

"You have to make it sound genuine in order for this to work."

Close my mouth. Someone find a needle and some string; I want to stitch my lips closed. Never again will I speak.

"Say it again," Spencer commands.

## I KILLED A MAN

He plays it back.

I hadn't noticed that he was recording me saying the words.

"Does that sound like someone who killed a man?"

Of course not.

Spencer sighs, "We either do this or we don't. Tell me now, what is it going to be?"

So someone that knew me would probably say that I'm not acting like myself. I have never been the type to go soft on something sinister; I am not a moralist. Not at all. I used to enjoy the way it felt to punch someone in the face. You might know me well enough to see that I haven't been myself since the first chapter. Then again, was that me, or just a permutation, some kind of performance? Where do I look, what do I find when I look in the mirror?

Willem Floures, I hear, has always been a bit of a rebel.

He goes against the so-called grain.

In addition to being a fighter, he used to be the calm and brooding being in interviews, the one that barely spoke but said more with his silence.

He was all of these things, but not lately.

Or, maybe, he's changed. He certainly fights using familiar signature moves and combinations. Depending on where you look, he's a young prodigy, a journeyman looking to redefine, or an old mainstay, rambling to himself, turning to sensationalism and big lies in order to maintain the audience's attention. Odds are that's him. Willem Floures.

When he says:

## I KILLED A MAN

He should mean it.

He shouldn't cower behind morality and other sorts of principles.

He should stop talking in the third person; he isn't that kind of stylist.

Yeah so I say it twice more, for Spencer's sake.

Each time it feels easier, more innate. Give it a little while longer and I might actually believe it.

Really though, I just want to rest. I want more painkillers.

I want to spar for a few rounds. Maybe fight through the pain long enough to feel nothing at all.

"I killed a man," and it sounds like something said at face value. I killed a man and tomorrow everyone will know about it.

## SILENCE

I get to talking about something else, about the house.

"You should think about repairing the roof."

Spencer shrugs, "Who's got time for that?"

Upstairs we hear a loud crashing.

Alarmed, I sit up.

"Relax," Spencer rolls his eyes, "it's James."

"Wait a minute, are you for real?"

A grin. Spencer says, "What do you think?"

"I thought it was just some imaginary friend of Sarah's."

He laughs, "Guess."

"I haven't a clue."

"I could be lying," Spencer narrows his eyes, "but it could also be true."

He says it again as if this is all one big lesson:

## YOU CAN LIE ABOUT THAT

"If you can't tell the difference, maybe it doesn't matter."

These are a trainer's words. He is trying to build me back up, trying to beat down all of the doubt that's boiled to the surface. And I'd thank him for it, but somehow I am still not certain that this will result in something we won't regret later. However, at the same time, I don't see how we can stop now.

It's already too late.

This is round two in a fight that probably never ends.

We fight until winded, and then we fight some more.

He's wrong about one thing.

You can't lie about that.

Can't say it's a fight you win because I'm not so sure anyone can win this particular fight. The opponent is time and its punches change you until they send you to the ground, six feet down and dead, the last brand of light isn't limelight, it's the bright light of the bare bulb hanging from above, the mortician tending to your body.

Somewhere in there, I feel like I'd still remain.

Unable to understand if I had died or not.

Win or lose?

## SILENCE

Neither of us says anything.

I keep my eyes closed. I listen to the house in pain, mimicking my own groans, the ache of each joint, the cuts and bruises that still need a lot of time to heal. I inhale, hold, and exhale before asking:

"Do you think I can go spar for a few rounds?"

Spencer looks up from the laptop, expression as if saying:

## WHAT THE FUCK DO YOU THINK?

It's a no-go.

And probably better that I just rest.

What about the painkillers?

I want to ask but all of a sudden it feels like an impossible question to pose; the silence of the house lulls me into a self-conscious cocoon.

I want to keep, and obey, the silence.

For awhile, it feels like I've escaped the world.

## SILENCE
## PERFECT
## SILENCE

But it ends around the same time Spencer starts typing again, and I can only imagine what else he is planning.

Whatever it is, you'll hear about it in the morning.

# THE SILENCE I REACH

As part of the plan, I keep my silence. I keep my silence despite having been more or less silent throughout most media events that have involved any part of me. Media events of silent intrigue and steady enigma. But silent especially now as I reach a new plateau of distance, carrying along a grimace, maybe a frown if it calls for it, favoring facial gestures that fit the design of the headlines around the time word got out.

And word certainly got out.

Stuff like:

'SUGAR' WILLEM FLOURES MURDERS HIS PAST

And:

BAR FIGHT GONE AWRY FAMOUS BOXER
SUSPECTED OF MURDER

I maintain my silence.

Spencer keeps me updated on all media requests.

We remain at the house, laptop against laptop, kitchen table our office, as I case off the painkillers and frequently hide from the steady current of suspicion with a few rounds in the ring Spencer installed in the basement.

My own private gym.

When your name is Willem Floures, you really can't afford to be seen in public gyms. Not because I'm smug (I'd never claim to have much of an ego; I'm too self-conscious to be egotistical) but because of the fact that the others like the same kind of gyms, same sort of equipment, same towns, cities, everything. For example, 'Buster' Willem Floures lives next door.

He is Spencer's neighbor. Neither party planned for it.

It just happens.

Seems 'Buster' liked the quiet, slightly rundown little suburb too.

I mean having my own private gym means everyone has their own private gym and only the media really suffers.

No media day workouts.

No public sparring sessions.

No open calls for opponents.

No surprise challenges.

Everything is under wraps. A shroud.

But they will do what we say if they want to be partners in news-stories and spectacle of the likes of SUSPECTED MURDER.

I can't say that I want it to fall into their hands, but then again who really has control over the media? Many claim they do and have the dollar signs to prove it; however, just so often a paid-for event hits public awareness. Something unexpected, like some nugget of information from a dark past resurfacing. In this case, I have killed a man that does not exist.

The media hears from the original source, Spencer posting under one of his longtime message board handles on boxing forums (boxing aficionados are some of the most vocal people around; they'll debate for dozens of pages about fight patterns, the dynamics of the power punch, and famous boxer career choices), mentioned this particular dark nugget from my "past."

It didn't take long for it to spread.

Spencer did more, of course. He had photos, doctored documented proof (medical records?)—

He had something.

I know he did. Kept me in the dark for obvious reasons.

**1)** I didn't want to know about it.

And—

**2)** I am supposed to plead ignorance/innocence.

## I CAN LAST THREE ROUNDS

Before I am gassed. This isn't even an actual fight. I'm merely working in some shadowboxing exercises while Sarah watches and pretends to be her father, shouting commands at me.

Think: Cliché of boxer trainer, "LEAD WITH THE JAB!"

Of course I lead.

It all comes from the jab.

I used to like doing this. Fighting.

Right?

Yeah.

Ask any of them and they'll all say yes.

## DO YOU LOVE BOXING?

NOTE: And all its variations such as "Do you like to fight?" and "Did you want to be a boxer?" and "Do you enjoy taking a punch?"

EXECUTIONER: Absolutely.

ICE: Wouldn't want to do anything else.

BUSTER: I guess so. I am a fighter aren't I?

ONE-TWO: That's a stupid question given that you're asking a professional boxer...

Yeah so I guess my answer would be an absolute, one hundred percent confident:

SUGAR: Yes!

Maybe drop the exclamation point...

## YES

Yeah that's better.

I can agree to disagree with myself. By the looks of it, I'm a bit of a hypocrite. You turn the page you see a different side of me. Maybe more of the same, but the subtleties (if I can be considered subtle) take on poor, imprecise shifts like someone that is constantly aching to be in the limelight...

But doesn't know why.

I'm afraid of the dark.

I am drawn to the brightest lights. Nothing is brighter than the lights shining on the ring on fight night.

Imagine the warmth of everyone's gaze.

Imagine that you are standing facing the only person that matters:

Yourself.

And you are prepared…

Prepared to go twelve rounds if need be. You will defeat that part of you that fights back. You will fight yourself, JAB JAB POWER SHOT if it takes all the blood and guts spilled to the canvas to get you to stay down.

Imagine that and you might begin to understand why fighting is all I can do. It's all I'm made to do. I understand the fight. Everything else, well that's sort of the issue here. I started fighting in hopes of finding myself; big surprise fighting only created more of a rift between each emotion, each resurrected feeling, I might have.

There are no easy identities, only more interesting proximities.

## CAN I GO ANOTHER ROUND?

Sarah seems to think so.

From upstairs I can hear Spencer laughing.

Things must be going well. But that's not my fight. Well, it is, but at this very moment, I want to be as far removed from the version of me they are sculpting. I will see myself imposed upon every possible mode-of-delivery.

A good rumor makes for great spikes in site-hits, subscription purchases, and so forth. I don't blame the media. They are the blood.

They carved out the veins.

No one exists without blood flowing.

The media makes sure the people that want to, need to, desire to be alive are still there, being viewed.

Read: Alive.

## YOU ARE ALIVE

Right now, I am because they say that 'Sugar' Willem Floures is a murderer. Right now, I am because I am lead subject on over a dozen media outlets' front pages. Right now…

I AM ALIVE because I lied.

Therefore, I am living a lie.

And not just one.

As many as needed.

Sarah asks me, "Do you want to win this?"

Words right from her father's mouth. Spencer always barked the question in raspy, throaty calls during my training sessions.

Motivation mostly, but you know what…

I have been so busy thinking about my chances of winning that I have failed to think about whether or not I want to win.

What is in it for me if I win except a rematch, another one that fights on their toes, quick to strike, ready to replace me?

## I WANT TO WIN

I know that I do but these days I worry that I don't have any other motivation, nothing else to claim as purpose, besides the victory. I want to win because I want to win.

"Yes," I shout back.

Sarah giggles, "JAB!"

Just like her father, she does her best to pretend that we have it all under control. But really, I'm in the basement, gassed, tired, achy, only a few days away from the rematch, and I haven't even begun to train.

I have become someone people can't stop talking about, not because I am still in their minds a great fighter but rather because I might be convicted. I might be *that person that killed some person*. When it involves murder, everyone gets at least moderately interested.

I lean back against the turnbuckle, corner of the ring my place to calm down, check my heartrate, and most importantly, listen for Spencer.

What is happening?

I tell Sarah, "Go get your father. Tell him we need an update."

She salutes me like a soldier, "Yessir!"

Carefree and not at all concerned with identity and placement in this society, Sarah might end up disappearing on her eighteenth birthday like so many others. Without a visible and brand-worthy identity (and unless you fix yourself to one) you disappear from society. You become brandless. You are just another person, faceless and making do.

I have always feared that sort of scenario.

However, when I see the anonymous so quick, so carefree, I often wonder if it was their choice. Their decision to be private. Their identity solely theirs, no one else's.

There might only ever be one Sarah Mullen.

Maybe she wants it to be that way.

That's a lot of pressure, being in full control of yourself.

How anyone can do that…I can't even begin to fathom.

Spencer has his own past. There are other Spencer Mullens out there. I know that a few of them have a Spencer as their trainer. They just don't let Spencer treat them the way he treats me.

I never got over my social anxiety.

I never got over the fact that people are watching me and they care and yet I still need to say something interesting, something poignant.

I settle for silence.


## SILENCE

It beats saying something you regret, something people won't forget.

Spencer with daughter descends the stairs.

"My, my," Spencer sounds chipper.

"You wouldn't believe…" he starts but then stops when he notices that I have boxing gloves on and I am noticeably sweaty.

"I didn't say you could start training."

"I needed something to keep my mind off the hysteria."

Spencer rolls his eyes, "This is the sort of spectacle that increases your brand." Sarah wanders over to the left corner of the ring and hangs on the ropes.

"Sarah quit that!"

I add, "Yeah you don't want to sprain your ankle."

Out of breath. This is bad.

"Look at you, you wasted all that energy."

"I have to train, Spencer."

"What did I say? Huh?"

I know what he said.

I know, I know. But a fighter trains before a big fight.

"It's hopeless. Every punch you throw is one less you can throw in the ring on fight night. Your training days are over. Now it's about fight psychology, staying attuned to your fighter instincts, and most of all: Eat healthy."

I throw a few jabs.

"Three down the shitter, right there."

"Only jabs, Spencer. This is helping me. It helps center me."

He sighs, "Wait until you hear about what they've done to you. You'll be brimming with confidence!"

## I BECOME THE PERSON VIEWED
## IN THE HEADLINES

Happy I have the boxing gloves and hands taped up otherwise I'd be compelled to scratch at my face. The media took the rumor and took on the remainder of Spencer's plan. It has reached the authorities and media consultant experts have been quoted saying things like "inconclusive" and "it is quite possible" while the story as a whole is shrouded in mystery.

It's because there is no data.

Nothing besides what Spencer knows and won't tell me.

(Thank you, I don't want to know.)

## EVERY BOXER REGISTERS THEIR HANDS
## AS WEAPONS

And I am no different.

You can train the human body to be a murder weapon.

My knuckles are split and scarred. If I were to punch a wall, I wouldn't feel much of anything. I'd leave a mark, the impact might break the skin, but, like I used to always say to fans during meet-and-greets (when I still had them; that's another worry— why haven't I been receiving any meet-and-greet requests?), what you don't feel can't hurt you.

## WHAT YOU DON'T FEEL CAN'T HURT YOU

Then you see how the following doesn't hurt.
It actually helps the 'Sugar' Willem Floures brand.
Let spill some media slander—

"How disgraceful!"

"Are we to think a professional can act in such a deplorable manner?!"

"This is no act of god."

"This is the problem with society: Its identity is rife with absolutes. Freedom is not an accessory. It is something you value and control!"

"Taking bets on the next great league…"

"It was a long time ago. We all make mistakes…"

"Can we really forgive him?"

"X must be worried."

"Praise a fighter for his failures and mistakes and you praise this crooked world for how numb it has become."

"Who said you can kill a person and get away with it? Oh, that's right—Floures."

"I used to watch every Floures fight. 'Sugar' stood out. He was the best of the best. Now I just don't know anymore…"

"We will see if the demons get their due."

"Executioner, you have yourself a criminal to cull."

The world is ripe with anger and hostility.

"It's a sight to behold," Spencer smiles.

The concerned and guilty version of me would start worrying, rambling about how this might backfire; the guilty version would go against what Spencer just showed me. Guilt has a way about shutting up if you shut down the right avenues of feeling. I unlace the boxing gloves. I yawn.

I work on unraveling the tape.

I don't say a word.

I picture the near future. I get into character.

Tap into the fighter, the 'Sugar' in Willem Floures.

I am seeing not hearing.

I am seeing not feeling.

Spencer is somewhere else, catering to the chaos of the lie. He will tend to it while I tend to nothing. I must get into character if I'm going to get through this. No thoughts about what's impending. No thoughts at all about how large portions of the audience will be watching because they hate me. The hate will fuel me; their hate will ensure a sold-out fight night.

I am seeing the future like it is the past.

I get into character, pretending that I haven't changed one bit.

So what if I lied?

## LIES

I can condition myself to see the vast array of a varied past.

The lies will lull me into a guilty sleep but I must stay awake.

Sarah carries the gloves away from me, stowing them in the locker down the hall. Spencer ascends the steps, "Got to get back to it. I'm about to submit a written interview. Hope you don't mind that I'm writing it as you. They wanted to speak directly to you. I would have asked you but..." he shrugs his shoulders, "you know."

I nod.

Centering myself.

Push that piece of information away. Not to be concerned.

I am seeing.

I am seeing:

## HEADLIGHTS

I am seeing that I can still focus in on the straight line, the angle of fight logic; I can still walk that long mile, that all-too-quick stroll from locker room to ringside. I can tune out the world while the world can't so much as tune into what I'm thinking. What are we thinking?

We are ready to fight.

Executioner, I know what you are thinking right now.

## ARE YOU READY?

It is almost time.

Does it bother you that I've murdered someone? Does it bother you that because I murdered someone, it means you did the same?

Willem Floures is a murderer.

We are currently under the scrutiny of the moralized public.

For however many that care, there are twice as many that expect one of us to end up on a stretcher after the rematch.

Blood will be shed.

## AT THE WEIGH-IN
## WHAT WILL YOU TELL ME
## THAT I DON'T ALREADY KNOW?

## ANYTHING LEFT WORTH SOME SURPRISE?

*There comes a time when it pays more to push rather than play along.*

Alone in the basement, I focus on the heavy bag.

That's you, Executioner.

I see only the light above as you fall to the canvas, spitting blood.

Commentators spouting hyperbole, shocked faces seen from where I stand in the corner, still hopping on my feet, spry as any one of you competitors thinking you can claim what I've built.

I see this in the comforted silence of this house.

Confidence is hard to come by, and at the moment I feel renewed.

Push it all away.

I won't play along.

I'll let the pieces play it out, and let it be known that Willem Floures killed a man because he had to. Self defense.

But that's not that interesting of a story.

He made a mistake.

He didn't mean to—CONFESSION and RECONCILIATION.

The public enjoys a good second-chance story.

## THE DARK PAST
## GIVES WAY
## TO FUTURE SUCCESS

How admirable.

I am seeing the glare of the headlights.

My eyes dry, and I wince, shutting them.

Mentality is everything.

But is it enough?

## SILENCE AND LAUGHTER

Really though, despite all that I see and have seen, I know I do this to spare myself the worry, the discomfort, of what's going on in the world.

The happenstance that happens to lay claim to the fact that Willem Floures is no pretty-boy, no professional with a clean record.

Just another identity tainted by criminal activity.

I push away the fact that it was my idea…

And more so the realization that I wouldn't be here, wouldn't be even remotely focused, on the rematch if it weren't for burying my clean record for the resurrected fiction of a bar-drunk and blackout murder.

The only thing left is to take solace in a theoretical fiction.

I think about X, and what I could still do to him. I sit in the corner of the ring, with the basement lights turned off, and I dream up a scenario where the person I killed was part of myself.

Executioner found dead with a blade through his eye.

The scenario is as pleasing as it is alarming. I can feel the blade puncturing my eye, made possible only by the power of the mind.

Who would mourn the loss more than me?

I'd enjoy his death for a time. I know I would. However, eventually I would feel like I'm missing something. Willem Floures is only as diverse as the parts that populate his personality.

If one perishes, are we any greater for it?

## I KILLED A MAN BUT WOULD ANYONE CARE IF I KILLED MYSELF?

In the dark, the silence takes me into a deep sleep.

When I wake up, Sarah tells me that it's morning outside. The hysteria has subsided enough to leave the house. And today is a big day.

Today is the weigh-in.

I grip the flab around my stomach.

## HOW MUCH WEIGHT HAVE I GAINED?

Weigh in my age, my lacking in pounds.

I wonder how much more baggage I'm carrying than Executioner.

Odds are, it'll be a topic-of-interest at the weigh-in.

They'll think about it, placing it in the perfect flabby folds of sensationalized and skewed fight analysis (favoring, of course, Executioner).

I only hope Spencer is right:

"They'll be too busy thinking about the murder to focus on the pounds."

# THE SILENCE I PREACH

The weigh-in is predictably a clustered wreck of flashing lights, loud noises, and various lobbying media peons looking to pull me aside for a sound bite, a quick interview, something. I stand behind a blockade of paid-for guards, these crewmembers paid by the event planner to make it appear like X and I have big training camps. Actually, it looks like X has a fairly substantial crew, an entourage to be more exact. But yeah…

It makes me look important having six guards wearing black pushing through the gathered masses.

I walk the stage; find my cue, a mark of tape, where I stand and wait.

X does the same.

And then it's lights, camera, *none of the above.*

Really it's not that exciting.

Spencer talks to himself. What might he be talking about? I haven't a clue. This whole thing is kind of simple. It doesn't need to be anything more than what it sounds—a weigh-in—but then again every opportunity to extract is an opportunity to create spectacle and it looks like the "agent" in Spencer is coming to life as he shouts in the face of the other, grimacing when it's his turn to shout back at Spencer. The cameras catch the little argument. So odd, then, when it fizzles, not amounting to much.

X and I refuse even a cursory glance.

Pretend we don't exist.

Stand and look serious.

Wait until we hear it.

AUDIENCE APPLAUSE

Suddenly it gets quiet.

This is the cue that the weigh-in is about to begin.

The challenger goes first. Me. So whatever but really I hate this part. I'm nervous. I pretend that I'm not. I frown, holding onto the scowl, the sincerest form of expressing hatred for myself, as I take off my mesh pants, my shirt, strip down to only the thinnest possible form of underwear we could manage.

I look horrible.

I know I do.

Do I still have any muscle tone?

Anyone actually impressed with the way I look?

### AUDIENCE SILENCE

It's the worst kind of silence.

I make a note of the fact that when I step up to the scale, when they weigh me, when I flex my arms, the flash from the crowd's cameras aren't nearly as blinding as they should be.

Instead of my gaze being washed white in the glow of so many camera shots, I can see into a large crowd as they stare back at me, equally unimpressed.

I have flab on my stomach.

Where muscle definition should be clean I have little jagged lines, perforations made to be the byproduct of fat existing right under the epidermis. That is flab. That is fat from a decade or more of not taking care of my body.

This is the body of a boxer that hasn't trained.

The training I have is the training of a man that's been through a lot but maybe not yet enough to have it all figured out.

Flex, close my eyes so that I don't see the number.

Tune out my surroundings so that when they declare my weight, I am elsewhere.

### WEIGHT AT...

Don't hear it.

### AUDIENCE APPLAUSE

I don't hear it, and I am ready to put my clothes back on. This is a beauty contest for broken beings. My body used to be cut to fit the make of a fighter, now my body is evidence of the fact that we cannot ever be the same.

We age.

We all change.

The lights dim as the cameras are set to ready.

X's turn.

## AUDIENCE APPLAUSE

Typically I don't watch because I don't want to confuse myself. The basic facts are enough to blur the lines of reality. How can I weigh so much when he can weigh so little? He makes weight without any problem.

I block out the fact that I might not have made weight.

I whisper, "Is it alright?"

Spencer sighs, "It'll do."

Not the kind of answer I wanted but…

## IT'LL DO

The place washes white as X flexes, makes the weight.

I notice that he has the same scar on his back, the same one that I had when I was younger but has since faded.

I notice that I'm watching and that this can't end well.

It involves a lot of self-scrutiny.

Watching, comparing, loathing.

Falling into myself, my own tendency to over-analyze becomes my cause to self-destruct.

Distantly, I know why Spencer isn't worried that I didn't make weight.

There will be a fight.

There will continue to be a number of battles. No one will deny the world a fight after what happens at the weigh-in.

## AUDIENCE APPLAUSE
## RATHER THAN

## AUDIENCE
## SILENCE

The camera flash lights up the room.

It's blinding from where I stand in the back, slowly removing myself from the scene with each step I take.

Spencer mouths the words:

## WHERE DO YOU THINK YOU'RE GOING?

I know but still.

And yet…

Umm…

Wait!

You see I want to—

Umm…

Someone take me out of this.

## AUDIENCE LAUGHTER

X said something that must have been funny, amusing.

At my expense?

Spencer beckons me to join him.

"Get the hell back here!"

I don't like this part of the weigh-in. This is where I pay my dues. This is where I do what needs to be done to generate buzz.

I walk up to X wearing that face.

Walk right up until we are close enough, our faces an inch apart.

Stare down.

## AUDIENCE SUSPENSE

What did you say to me?

What did you say to me?

Those are the words that need to come out of my mouth with certainty, with the volition of a madman wanting his title back.

"What did you say to me?"

Spencer whispers into my ear, "Either you set the tone or you don't make it to fight night. Your choice."

He's right.

This is not the time to be so hesitant and confused. I might not have control over myself but at the very least I can play the basic role of "fighter." I can pretend to care. I can wear that face.

I can gamble away whatever cards I have yet to play.

Fine.

"Say it," I shout.

"Fucking say it!"

## AUDIENCE SUSPENSE

And I am the cause of the suspense.

X grins, doing his best not to be intimidated. Truth is he probably isn't and finds this charade to be predictable, but he plays along too.

The weigh-in is a popularity contest.

Who lights up the room the brightest?

X with his reply:

YOU
CAN'T
BEAT
ME
OLD
MAN

Still wearing that scowl, I whisper so that only X can hear: "You'll have to do better than that. Set the stage you shit."

I lob another line, this time louder:

YOU HAVEN'T BEEN IN AS MANY WARS AS I'VE BEEN, KID

YOU HAVEN'T A CLUE HOW HARD THIS SKULL OF MINE IS

# YOU WILL HAVE TO CRACK IT TO SEND ME TO THE CANVAS

I want him to push me.

I want him to take a step back.

I want this confrontation to cause him discomfort. He is already annoyed, already bothered by the MURDER. Being this close, right in his face, naturally encroaches upon that feeling that you're losing your cool.

I know him.

I know enough about him to know that this is one of the worst feelings in the world:

Being called out in front of such a large crowd.

Spencer brings me a cinderblock that has been treated to collapse to pieces with a swift strike.

Do you know what I'm about to do?

I have to break from the stare down in order to take the cinderblock but the inclusion of something like this at a weigh-in is unusual and as a result they light up the room brighter than I could have imagined.

I get high off the attention.

The fact that it is working gives me enough confidence to send my head careening against the cinderblock.

It breaks but not without breaking the skin.

Tearing it open right where I had been torn open in the last fight.

I scream, I shout, I choose to gamble…

YOU

CAN'T

HURT

ME

And it looks like I win.

It is caught on camera and it will be played back on all major venues.

A little alarming though to find it so easy, so one-sided. X didn't choose to fight back. When I'm afraid, I tend to make excuses. He didn't make any. His silence alarms me. Did I really intimidate him?

I cared more about the reaction from the audience.

*This old fighter can still break some faces.*

That's all I hoped to get across.

Seems the gamble paid off. And then some.

The fact that I killed a man warmed them up. The fact that I don't care about my health sends them over the edge.

AUDIENCE SILENCE
IS AUDIENCE SUSPENSE
IS AUDIENCE APPEASED

Executioner looks over his shoulder right before leaving the stage.

It's a look that kicks over the house-of-cards charade I had built all along. It's a look that says:

You're running on fumes.

It's a look that says:

Nice try.

It's a look that says:

You are going to lose and everyone knows it.

And he's right.

THIS ISN'T GOING TO BE MUCH OF A FIGHT

I want to fast-forward through the fight, all twelve rounds, just so that I can find out how bad I'm hurt when it's over. The cinderblock breaks into clumps, loose, like chalk; Executioner's signature strike to my old and busted cranium will do far more damage. I want to skip forward and somehow find out that I won. Everything will be okay. Executioner knocked out cold. Somehow I knock out a younger version of me.

Me: 'Sugar' Willem Floures with his oh-so-impressive twelve wins by KO.

Knock X out.

Who has won most of his fights by knockout.

How can that be?

It's because he's changing things. He's learned how to correctly sit down on his punches and maximize the precision of every landed punch.

## DON'T LAUGH

A person can change every part of himself.

At any given point in time we can take a picture and capture the person you were at that very moment; however, a dozen blinks later, the picture might no longer be accurate.

You might gain weight, gain insight; lose weight, lose a whole lot.

People change. You will change too.

You got to wonder what must it take to remain precisely the same, in the image wanted and expected.

## DON'T LAUGH

Because I've tried my best to remain the same.

I can't say that I like who I am but at the very least I've gotten this far. One of my biggest worries is "losing it." Whatever that means. I don't know how it happens but I've seen it happen.

It is happening to me.

*Shh.*

It's okay.

I admit it.

It is happening to me.

Losing whatever it is that made things bearable.

Give it enough time and your grip on that shade of reality will loosen.

Of course, I'm saying this mostly because I need to say it. No one needs to hear it more than me. I admit it and I say that I admit it but that's not actually true. All hot air...more bullshit, just like the lies I've used.

Just like that cinderblock.

Just like the fact that the murder is a fake.

It's bullshit. Treated to be spectacle, made to generate enough light to wash out every part of me that might be in contention.

Wash them all out.
Leave only the basic fact:
That I am 'me.'
I made this all possible.
This league wouldn't be as popular as it is if it weren't for me.

## WATCH ME

Everyone used to look forward to watching me.
Sure I basically just beat the shit out of myself but that was entertainment for the masses. They liked seeing my skills put to the test. Fight after fight, I wasted away my youth and my health but at the very least I sold out arenas, I moved products, I gained a number of endorsements.
I was at the peak of popularity.
Willem Floures.
Household name.
Solid gold, certified celebrity.
People would bow down if I dabbled in egocentricism and forced them to treat me like a god.
But you see I never got comfortable.

## LOOK AWAY

I always worried and never enjoyed my success.
How many have been washed out?
How much does this hurt?
Will I remember anything ten years from now?
My memory lapses…
Are they an indication of my passing?
When people talk about retirement do they mean to say that I am not Willem Floures and maybe I never was?

## BIGGEST WORRY
## WORST SOUND

Their laughter, directed at me.
They are all nameless, strangers not confidants, family, or

friends, and yet that somehow makes it far worse. I want their approval.

I want to make sure that this weigh-in means more to them than it does to me. I don't know where to divide and draw the line, which is why I have made a career out of hurting myself. Who does that?

Fighters are considered to be athletes.

And yet...

I see myself standing there, on the other side of the ring, and I always think the same thing:

## WHO IS THAT?
## WHO ARE YOU?

I look at that person like it's someone else.

I look at myself in the mirror and confuse the reflection for a person I haven't yet met.

My memory lapses...my mind erased...

With every fight I begin to wonder if the oddity and inconsistency of my words, my voice, my life, my choices, my actions aren't one long ramble.

I begin to wonder if any of this is real.

And then I feel foolish.

I tell myself, "Get real."

Because it is very real.

What's about to happen.

This isn't going to be something that I second-guess. Really, if I were truly prepared, there would be no guessing.

## READY OR NOT

I would be prepared enough that I wouldn't need sleeping pills the night before the fight. I would be prepared enough that I could keep cool, my mind never wandering back to the impending fight.

No nausea. No anxiety.

I would be myself.

And I wouldn't follow up that statement with the words

"whatever that means."
I would know.
See that person across the ring?
It's me.

## WILLEM FLOURES

We get paid to fight. People watch us fight and marvel at the mastery of each punch thrown, shudder and cringe when they hear a punch landing against our body, aimed right at our skull. The blood splatter sometimes traveling out of the ring to the immediate vicinity at ringside, they pay top-dollar on online auction sites for blood-splattered garb stained and authentically signed by me, by us, after the fight.

We get paid to fight and the world around us develops a second and third party economy. The industry of the fight:

We last as long as we need.

We last as long as we can.

## GETTING AHEAD OF YOURSELF THERE

Really though, I shouldn't be able to speak for myself. I'll only end up losing the point halfway through. I write down most everything worth remembering. Sound advice—keeping a log of information—but what no one ever realizes is that it's equally worthless if you keep forgetting where you put the log. I've lost so many lists of facts and information about myself that it has become a bit of a joke.

I anticipate finding them long after they are lost.

It'll be like discovering correspondence from the person I once was.

Log of the identity known as 'Willem Floures's complete with run-on sentences and an unfamiliar voice ringing out in my head like a moralist:

## HOW COULD YOU?
## HOW DO YOU DO THIS?
## SELLING YOURSELF

## HURTING YOUR BODY
## FOR THEIR AMUSEMENT

But then it's funny because in one of those logs, I believe I'd find a better answer than I could conceive at a moment's notice.

Something wise and clever like:

"Don't we all sell ourselves to seem more important?"

Or—

"We sell a part of ourselves just so that we know what's at stake during the lost-and-found of our lives."

Needless to say, I haven't found any of the logs.

It's like the moment I finish they cease to exist.

I only hope I won't cease to exist before leaving something behind as confirmation, something that proves that I was 'Willem Floures.'

*Incapable of being replaced.*

*The one the only.*

*That kind of stuff.*

*Extremely sentimental and positive statements from people that knew me and/or loved my fights.*

*No attention paid to my many failures.*

*No attention paid to the parts of me that are left behind.*

*He was, past tense, the greatest.*

*He was, past tense, Willem Floures.*

In passing the name is rendered a past remembrance.

That's what I want and I know that it's impossible.

Willem Floures will live on.

## SORRY

My mind tends to wander.

Right before a fight, I have to let my mind wander if I don't want to psych myself; if I focus on the fight for too long, I forget why I'm fighting.

I forget who I am.

And that already happens way too much.

So I preach the silence that comes with the territory of being scatterbrained. I intentionally lose myself in thought, sitting

alone for long durations, staring off into space.
I am not here.
I can't be.
Not tonight.
Save it for the ring.
Tell myself:
*Shh.*

## YOU KNOW WHO YOU ARE

# VERSUS

True sign of a manic mind: Moments before I'm confident and self-assured, only to pick up where we left off: doubt.

## WHO DO YOU THINK I AM?

It's those cursory signals, hearing the click and the boom of the arena lighting up with anticipation, that equally manic sense of anticipation:

Electricity.

I shadowbox to do something, to fill the time, to get my heart rate up in the fifteen minutes, half hour before the fight. Really though, my mind is floating, my gaze nowhere near the glow of a focused fighter. I might as well be sitting down next to Spencer, next to the few paid-for crewmembers, including an extremely expensive cutman, because as Spencer said:

"Your skin tears like paper. Last thing we want is having the fight stolen from us via TKO."

Really, I watch myself shadowbox, voyeur to my own actions.

The locker room is silent; brooding out from underneath the silence is the impending laughter and cheer of the audience.

Hear it.

Feel it.

Nothing.

I wish that were true.

I settle on the one-two jab followed by a right or left hook.

JAB
JAB
HOOK

There it is: My strategy.

Other than clinching, I don't have much else except the buildup of psychological residue that I know isn't working on someone like Executioner. It wouldn't have worked on me back when I was his age.

We can hear the ground shaking from the audience erupting in applause as the previous fight seemingly ends.

"Turn on the TV," I tell one of the crewmembers.

"No," Spencer shakes his head.

## STAY FOCUSED

I want to see who won. 'King Crown' Willem Floures or 'Gallows' Willem Floures? It should have been a close fight. At that age, I would have been desperate for the KO. Anything to gain some regard. We're all the same except that somewhere during their first fifteen fights, their career took a wrong turn. Instead of climbing the league ladder, they stopped climbing.

They became journeymen.

Gatekeepers.

Basic examples of who I am, plus or minus a few addictions.

I always had an addictive personality. It comes with the territory of being Willem Floures. In Gallows's case, he got into painkillers. He got in them bad, real bad. I know the feeling of being pulled into the nonspace of relaxation and half-thought. In that space, there is no such thing as poor thought. Nothing fazes you. It feels about as real as you want it to feel; everything else floats by as something fake, nonessential.

I'd love to float on by without any rhyme or reason for holding onto the professional identity I've fixated on for decades.

But I can't.

Like the act of fighting, I am always inundated by the bothersome consequences.

## I MIGHT LOSE

There's a large possibility that I'll lose.

And as we get word that it's time, someone with a headset

knocking on the locker room door at the same time Spencer receives a call from one of the event producers, they give us word:

"Two minutes until you begin the walk."

Spencer nods.

The producer holds up two fingers, "Two!"

Leaves without looking me in the eye.

## THE WALK

It sounds exactly like what it is:

The locker rooms are usually recessed deep within the arena, far enough away from the action to provide enough solace from the energies that often ruin your mood, spoiling your entire fight strategy, but as a result, you have that longest walk to the ring. It's a walk that usually centers a well-trained fighter and derails the fighters that are not ready for this.

*This.*

Spencer with the expected:

## READY?

A question with no real answer.

A slight sweat generated from shadowboxing, not quite out of breath but not quite fresh either, I stand in place, shifting my weight from left to right while Spencer checks my gloves, the lacing tight enough, covers me with my signature "Sugar Gold" robe.

I hide under the hood of the robe and as I take the first steps, initiating the long walk to the ring, I stare not ahead but at the ground.

Turning the corner, they wait for me. They wait for me wherever they can get the clearest shot. Flicker, within frame:

The media takes pictures, captures footage, tagging it all not in expectation of the future victor but rather as the man walking the long walk to his execution and his opponent the sworn Executioner.

Gaze to the ground.

I walk, separating sense from self.

In a dozen steps, I watch from behind, the steady rhythm of the walk culminated with the pressure of twelve rounds ready to end my career.

Fight. Stand up and fight.

Fight all of these negative thoughts.

There's more to the fight than the minutes, the hour, in the ring. The fight began the moment the first picture was taken of me in relation to the rematch. The fight has been ongoing and I won a round while losing three.

I won via lying about murder.

I won via the staging of a shattered cinderblock.

But together, I have lost more rounds than I've won simply due to the inability to control the measure of my thoughts.

If I lose, it's because I can't get outside of myself.

If only I could watch from where I linger, right at this moment, the rhythm affording the ability to watch from afar, my slumped over shoulders already projecting defeat.

If only this level of focus could be maintained.

## IT CAN

But will I?

Again, I battle doubt and guilt and something else.

"Something else" is reserved for all that I cannot even begin to explain. You probably see it better than I do.

What do you see?

Oh, wait:

Don't talk to me.

I turn the last corner, the long walk growing shorter.

I can hear my entrance music.

As always it's generic death metal. Predictable but that's what 'Sugar' walks out to and that's how it'll end.

## IF THIS IS MY LAST FIGHT

I watch as I stretch my back, throw a few punches, hopping in place as I stop momentarily at the curtain.

I crack my neck.

Center, find your center…
It is now or never.

## WASHED WHITE

Light.
All I see as I push through the curtain out towards the ring.
And I walk.
The longest walk of all.
The one to the ring.

## NOISE

The audience is a mixture of cheers and leers, curiosity and hatred for this old fighter, a fighter that will do anything to win. And they know it. Believe me they know it. The audience is smarter than you think. Question is, do they know that I deal in lies? Do they know what it takes to stay in the bright light?

My focus is the ring. I look nowhere else.

Throw a few punches, for effect. Tune into the music being buried by the boos and other rambling noise.

I see the banners hanging from above.

They used an older picture of me for the official fight card. Something in me cracks, wilts, a flutter of the nerves. Everywhere I look I can't avoid what waits for me.

## IF THAT'S HOW IT'S GOING TO BE,
## THAT'S HOW IT'S GOING TO BE

I strafe around the ring twice, raising my arms, posing for the cameras. Media afire with various shots, the arena rumbles, the air feels thick, hard to take in. Every inhale takes something out of me. The atmosphere of a fight. I stare at the other side of the ring, where Executioner will soon stare me down, waiting for his chance to send another uppercut right where it'll end me.

My music stops, replaced by X's droning hip-hop track.

The audience switches modes, negative to positive, as X runs to the ring alone. His crew about two minutes behind, walking slowly, not at all worried that X will be winded by the audacious sprint to the ring.

I would have done something like that when I was his age.

I didn't, but I could have.

Easy to say that you "would" or "could" have done something but hey, hey, X has entered the ring. Need to *not* be in my own head right now.

He stands front and center, flexing his arms, snubbing me entirely.

The music dies down. The referee takes his spot and so too does the announcer.

Time for hyperbole…

## TIME FOR INTRODUCTIONS

The announcer shouts into the microphone:

"Tonight, we are going to witness one of the most important matches in the history of professional boxing…

"Are you ready?

"Boxing fans, are you ready…?

"For the thousands in attendance, and the millions watching at home, ladies and gentleman…

"It's time for fight night!

"Twelve rounds for the proof of being the best of the best!

"Introducing first, fighting out of the blue corner, wearing solid black trunks with red trim…'Executioner' Willem Floures!"

## AUDIENCE UNANIMOUS APPLAUSE

"And in the red corner, wearing the gold trunks with white trim…'Sugar' Willem Floures!"

## AUDIENCE APPREHENSION
## MODERATE APPLAUSE

Tune it out.

We step forward, the referee goes through the usual rules.

"Touch gloves," to which we both choose to remain focused,

gaze digging as deep into X's eyes as I can.

Back to our own respective corners.

The tragic few seconds before the bell rings.

## ROUND ONE

Soon it is here, and I can already see the fight a few actions into the future. I remain on the defensive. X wants me to create opportunities for him, testing me with the jab, which this early into the fight, I can easily absorb. His jabs graze my gloves but do their job at keeping me shelled up.

I look for opportunities.

I find none so I throw out the jab, hoping to create one.

The round progresses the same way:

JAB

JAB

JAB

JAB

Trading jabs, absorbing them; in my case, I maintain my defensive shell. X moves around the ring on the balls of his feet, semi-circling me with his arms down. He teases out an opening, just one opening is all he needs to send me to the ground and we both know it.

I know what he's thinking.

I know that he's pissed about what I've done.

I'm not sure it was the greatest of ideas, but it's too late now. What's done is done. What makes it both good and bad at the same time is the fact that no one can expose the truth to the media without being hurt in the process. If X told the media the truth, that I never killed anyone, that it was a slanderous lie, he would reap the negative effects too.

This is why he wants to level me, send me down to the canvas early in the fight.

But not this round.

We return to our corners.

Spencer says something that I can't hear because I'm way too focused. I can't even look away from X. My gaze trained to him in his corner, never once looking away.

## ROUND TWO

I remain in my shell, occasional jabs.

He gets his work rate up with a few jabs and some decent hooks to the body that I fail to block. I hear it in my breath, the pain, wheezing from impact.

He quickly notices that if he continues landing a few hooks, I am unable to do anything. I cannot even throw out the jab. With every hook, I become more and more tired, gassed.

I don't want to do what I know to do.

It is the reason for fights to turn ugly and dull; however, it is the exploitable tactic of the tired fighter in denial.

I clinch, grabbing him, pulling him in, landing a few punches to the kidneys whenever I can get away with it.

X mutters, "You fuck!"

As I land a nice sharp one to his left kidney.

The referee breaks the clinch.

"Fight!"

Shouts in my face, a warning not to keep clinching. We're all seeing the fight a number of moves ahead. That's exactly what I'm going to do.

He tries for a combination but I grab his arm, pulling him in for another clinch. Three more like this and it's the end of round two and you can hear the audience:

## AUDIENCE BOOING

Spencer splashes water in my face, "The hell you doing?! Ease off the clinch. Vary it up with combinations! Save your energy!"

Sound advice but I'm still not listening.

Still staring at X, I mouth the words "I…will…kill…you."

Psychological mind games.

Whether or not it'll actually work, it's worth it. It works for me. I feel like I have some control over the fight and as I clinch my way through rounds three and four, much to the audience's dislike (everyone disgusted with such an anticlimactic fight) I begin to fall into a groove, one that vouches for doing whatever it takes to win.

To remain where I am.

It doesn't start now. It's already begun. I will do whatever it takes.

Don't you get it?

By round five, X is really frustrated.

## ROUND FIVE

This is where I get the warning from the referee, "If you clinch again, I will end the fight!"

## AUDIENCE APPLAUSE

X with a sly grin. That damn mouth guard that says "DIE" on it.

Taunt me all you want.

In this moment, I am confident.

I break through my shell with the jab.

X blocks, using fanciful footwork to stand just out of reach of my strikes. He turns to the audience, flexing and shouting.

They are all on his side.

For all they care, I'm a "nobody."

He is Willem Floures.

I'm some article from a different era.

I land a shocking hook to his face. It surprises him.

He switches to the defensive as I continue jabbing, thrilled to have caught him with the sort of punch I no longer knew I had.

Not a signature. Not anymore.

I'm just throwing punches, running on fumes.

## ROUND SIX

I am gassed but the experience of so many fights carries me on through the onslaught of this round and the next.

X unloads on me, combination after combination.

## AUDIENCE LAUGHTER

That cuts and stuns me harder than any of his strikes when he lands a straight shot to the body that sends me to the ropes, bouncing back, flying right into another shot.

He hasn't landed the uppercut yet.

He's waiting.

I know him.

Not a whole lot of patience unless it's recognized that everything is on the line. I think of what I might do to psychologically toy with him and give me another nudge in the right direction, the direction of a centered mind.

## ROUND SEVEN

There is an idea brewing in this brain of mine.

I go back into my shell.

I think about when it might be the right time.

Not now, next round.

X unloads throughout round seven and at one point I start tasting copper, blood now oozing from my mouth.

Unpleasant but not unexpected.

Shell, condensed, losing on the cards.

For now…

## ROUND EIGHT

I settle on the idea and take a knee.

The referee jumps between us, holding X back.

I expect the whole world to be in shock, wondering what did it. What stunned Sugar?

I have the one knee down, gaze to the canvas, waiting until I reach the six count to stand back up. The referee grabs me by the gloves, holds them, looks into my eyes, "You okay?" is what he's saying but not really meaning. This is just another day at the office. For him, he'd rather I stay down.

Why waste any more time?

I wait until the end of round eight to fake a low blow.

I do my best to act like I've been hooked to the groin. X shrugs his shoulders, shaking his head, shouting, "You've got to be fucking kidding me!"

This is so unlike me.

Well, how about that—

I can change too.

I do what needs to be done. I have my values but winning is everything. If I don't win this I won't be myself anymore.

Distantly I recognize that I have already let that one go:

Being true to oneself.

I would never fight dirty.


ROUND NINE


It's not over yet. I start with the jab again. X is irritated and annoyed which helps me win on the cards during this round.

This works:


JAB

JAB

JAB

STRAIGHT TO THE FACE


My shots might not be as quick or as punishing as his but X has lost his strategy. I've successfully derailed his linear path towards knockout.

Forty seconds left in the round I fake another low blow.

I keel over, mocking him even more as he turns to the audience, shouting "WHAT FUCKING BULLSHIT!"

But I'm not so sure the audience is on his side anymore.


AUDIENCE SUSPICION

WHERE IS IT AIMED?

AT ME?

AT HIM?


I'm okay and the referee makes sure that I'm okay before

letting the clock run out on the round.

Spencer in the corner asking me curiously, "You know what you're doing right?"

He's calm, an indication that he sees that something working.

The fight isn't a pretty one.

## BUT IT'LL DO

Water splashed over my face as the bell sounds.

## ROUND TEN

The fight can stand to look a little dirtier. When I clinch I make it look like X is doing all the clinching.

X goes silent, slows down, pressure placed on the act of fighting rather than the true expression of the fight, renders him confused.

He has never fought like this before. He has never experienced a fight where it isn't just the cards but rather the weight of each intended block that might turn the fight.

The fight is more or less directionless and yet there will be a winner.

*There will be a winner.*

I clinch throughout the round, throwing some punches right before to make it look like X is doing the grabbing.

The referee pulls him aside.

## A WARNING

Think about what the commentators must be discussing.

I glance over at their table situated at ringside.

They wear straight faces. Very little is being said.

## ROUND ELEVEN

This round will go down as the turning point in the fight.

I punch him low enough to hit his groin but high enough so that it doesn't appear to be an illegal shot. The referee doesn't see it. The audience doesn't see it. The cameras don't capture it and therefore it didn't happen.

It is legal.

And X falls to the ground.

## AUDIENCE SHOCK

I get a nine count.

You get punched in the groin hard enough and it's stunning, really, to see a man make it in time to keep fighting. I nearly had it won.

Confidence boost.

The rest of the round he isn't very active. What can he do other than rely upon recently obtained anger?

I toy with him. A clinch whenever he tries anything more than a jab.

The round ends and it's mine.

Spencer laughs, "Wow, just wow. I don't recognize you out there. You are fighting as someone else."

His would-be compliment comes off as a threat.

What does he mean I'm fighting as someone else?

Who am I if not someone familiar?

## ROUND TWELVE

X goes all out, flurries of punches and more than a few stun me.

I shell up, mind elsewhere, focus fractured, preoccupied with Spencer's comment. The round doesn't end well. Stunned, he gains a knockdown.

I take my time getting back up, eight count.

I stand there, glaring at him, and it's captured on camera. The look on my face reads: "Not impressed."

With a minute left I do my best to send a hook low enough to land another shot.

X applies pressure using a traditionally effective combination:

## JAB

JAB
HOOK
JAB
HOOK
UPPERCUT

He doesn't land the uppercut.

When I see the opening coming, I lean in, letting the jab hit me, and I say to him, "Hey...I know you..."

And this time, I send the uppercut, but not before landing a low blow.

The cameras only see the uppercut, the one that sends him to the canvas.

Saved by the bell?

Not in this league.

The referee starts the count.

## THE AUDIENCE IN APPLAUSE

In this moment, I feel content.

I forget what I had to do in order to remain in contention. I feel like myself. I repeat it over and over, "I'm Willem Floures," while watching part of me stumble around the ring, legs knocked out from under him.

But he stands up.

The referee looks into his eyes.

And that's the end of the fight.

Not a knockout.

## THE VERDICT

We wait for the judges' scores but already I see it all falling back in on me. I feel a great numbing pain in the back of my throat, unaware that I am biting into my tongue, my molars shredding it, all too consumed with what I know to be the conclusion.

## WINNER BY SPLIT DECISION

The name given, it isn't mine.

"~~Sugar.~~"

Figure the X on the marquee paid handsomely for the betting crowd, the warm wads of green bribery handed under the table, passing hands between one opportunist to another, bookie to judge and vice versa.

Who am I to judge the already judged?

What isn't dirty, what hasn't been lowered in order to leap higher?

## UNDERBELLY

And in this moment, I no longer have any standards.

It has always been personal.

But now—

*I will create the laughter.*

I will create the momentum.

I will become the exact opposite of everything they know about themselves. I will change what it means to be Willem Floures so much that they will be fighting in a league entirely their undoing.

Not just you X, but every single one of you.

Every part of me will be confused.

I will infuse a new identity, one that is about winning.

For so long, I have taken the personal as professional.

For so long, I looked at myself as a leader, best of the best because there was always something left to reinforce, to further understand and define.

Challenge myself.

Understand myself.

For so long, that was how I treated my career.

I looked for the true identity, unaware of the fact that the identity of Willem Floures was always shifting and changing.

They were applying their own textures.

Well now I change us.

I turn us into everything the world cannot help but watch.

# I TAKE IT PERSONALLY

And Executioner, *I know you...*
Do you know me?
Because if you did, you would see what's happening next.

# THE LAUGHTER I LOVE

*This is worth a laugh.* Spencer hugs Sarah, kneels down and, at eye-level, he tries to calm her down, "Why don't you go back upstairs? Isn't James supposed to be reading you a bedtime story?"

Sarah looks up at me, "Why is he laughing?"

Spencer tilts his head to one side, "Sometimes people laugh when they are nervous or worried."

"Why is he nervous?"

Sarah pleads with Spencer, hoping for a sincere explanation, one that he will not give. Try this instead, "He's nervous about society."

Sarah, typical inquisitive child, with her rejoinder, "Why is he nervous about society?"

Spencer holds back a sigh, "Society needs a reason, but do you sweetie?"

"Yes," Sarah whines.

"Oh, go on upstairs. Be a good girl. I can tell that you're tired. Look at those dark spots under your eyes…"

Sarah frowns but concedes; each step is an exaggerated stop up the staircase. "He's just nervous?"

"Yes, he's nervous."

"Why is he nervous?"

Looking at me, Spencer shouts to Sarah at the top of the stairs, "You know, I'm not so sure."

### SILENCE

I cover my mouth, suppressing laughter.

The sound of a door, opening and closing, the creaking of its hinges followed by the healing silence of the house.

I exhale and the house exhales.

Spencer points at the smile worn prominently across my face, "What? What is this shit, huh?"

## LAUGHTER
## MY LAUGHTER

Between lapses the house seemingly contracts, clutching every word escaping my mouth, like I shouldn't be saying this, shouldn't be having this conversation. I won't be able to take it back when all is said and done.

This is a conversation not worth having.

This is a conversation that I can't let pass.

"You..." and a little giggle, suppressed. "You...fucking kidnapped Executioner..."

Spencer doesn't find it amusing. In fact, he is neither angry nor frustrated. He is calm. "Yes. I did."

"You kidnapped...the champion..." Choke on my laughter.

Spencer nods.

Nonchalant about it: "I have him tied up in the basement, arms and legs bound and immobile. He won't make so much as a noise. I've made sure of it."

"What did you do?"

"Oh," Spencer shrugs, "nothing. His mouth is taped shut. Kept the mouth guard in there too. He couldn't work the tape free using his jaw or teeth if he wanted to."

My laughter turns into a long sigh, "Did I say you could do this?"

Spencer walks over to the basement door. He grips the doorknob, "You were the one that said it." Right before venturing downstairs, he narrows his gaze, "You said it first, remember?"

## "I KILLED A MAN."

"What did you say?!" I follow him down into the basement.

Sure enough X is plastered against the wall with tethers that stretch his appendages in such a way that it looks like it hurts. Duct tape in layers wrapped around the entirety of his face. Spencer left the blindfold off.

So that X may see everything.

So that I will be unable to escape his judging gaze.

Spencer grabs X's face, "You don't trust me?"

"What? What are you talking about?"

"*You* don't trust me."

"If you imply that I don't trust him, no I don't. Why would I?"

Pretending to move X's taped mouth, "You don't trust *me*."

"Listen, this can't end well. And, really, how did you even manage it?"

"Nurse your wounds. Leave it to me. You don't need to understand everything." Spencer punches X in the stomach. X makes little more than a muffled noise.

"This is insurance."

## INSURANCE?

Another punch. That one had to hurt.

"Makes for a good training dummy! Try it!"

Clenching my fists, I stand there, aware of what this means. Willem Floures cannot simply disappear. People will notice.

They might have already noticed.

"Don't you find that to be a problem?"

Spencer shrugs, "You are the one that killed a man."

"I didn't kill a man!"

Switching to the tone he saves for lectures, Spencer steps into the ring with me, "But you said it. We made it so. The media believed it. They believed it. Doesn't matter if it's fact or fiction. *They* believed it!"

"They are going to be looking for him…"

## THAT'S THE POINT

*Let them look.*

"You want them to find worse, much worse."

Spencer leans on the ropes, pretends to shadowbox.

"I do?"

## YOU SAID IT

"What did I say?"

Spencer seems to understand something that I don't and that bothers me. He's my agent; he is supposed to drone on and keep me in the loop.

"Shouldn't you, umm, lecture me about it or something?"

Spencer sighs, throws a few jabs, lowers his chin, gets into proper fighting stance, "You lectured me. Don't remember?"

## WHAT?

"What if I don't?"

Spencer lowers his fists, looks over at X, "He's here. He's listening. If he ever gets out, you don't want him knowing about your 'big plan.'"

## WHAT BIG PLAN?
## WHAT IS GOING ON?

"Don't act so confused, Sugar; you started it. I'm simply making sure it continues."

Back to shadowboxing. I step in the way of one of his jabs.

It hits me right in the nose, my vision cloudy, causes me to sneeze.

Spencer plays dumb, "You can still take a punch, huh?"

"Just. Fucking. Stop. Moving. Okay?"

Spencer raises an eyebrow, "Don't trust me?"

The way he says it, it's like he's hiding something. He is trying to get me to say something…but what?

I feel like I'm the only one not in on this big joke.

"What is going on, Spencer?"

"I'm not following." He raises his fists.

I grab one, "Stop. You aren't a fighter."

He looks me right in the eye and says:

## ARE YOU?

That one hits deep. My stomach knots and I can feel my grip tighten, crushing Spencer's hand.

This is about the last fight.

This is about the fight before last.

This is about what's happened the last few weeks.

This is not about me. It's about him.

I look over at X, who is watching everything happen.

Spencer looks down at my hand gripping his wrist.

I see it in his eyes.

"Hurts huh?"

Spencer sighs, "What if it did?"

"Out with it."

"What?"

"You are trying to blackmail me."

## LAUGHTER

I let go of his wrist.

I push him against the ropes and punch him lightly in the face.

He falls to the canvas, laughing harder than before.

"What's so fucking funny?!"

He gags on the sting of the punch.

"Huh?!"

"Don't you love it?"

I breathe heavily, watching Spencer climb back up to his feet.

"Don't you love it?" He laughs right in my face. "Don't you *love* the laughter?!"

## THE LAUGHTER

Tears run down my face.

At the sight of them, he points and laughs, "Don't you trust me?!"

I manage to say, after wiping away the tears, "If this is about the last fight, I did what I had to do. Sorry if I didn't follow your strategy."

Suddenly his face straightens and in clear monotone, Spencer says, "It has and always will be your story. I am merely a part of it."

## WHAT THE FUCK IS THAT SUPPOSED TO MEAN?

"You love the laughter," Spencer chuckles, the laughter starting up again. He walks to the other side of the ring and points to the opposite corner.

"Let me guess, you want me to stand there."

"Don't you trust me?"

Oh Jesus, what the hell is this?

Whatever, fine.

I stand in the corner.

## LOOKING FOR SOME ANSWERS

"The answers are right in front of you, Sugar."

"I expect you to help me find them," I warn him. "Otherwise, why else would I keep you around?!"

I instantly regret what I said.

But that's too late.

## THIS IS A CONVERSATION THAT'S A LONG TIME COMING

## THIS IS A CONVERSATION THAT CHANGES A FRIENDSHIP

It doesn't seem to affect Spencer. But I know him. I know how he thinks more so than I know myself.

"You don't trust me," Spencer announces.

He falls into a fighting stance. Approaches the middle of the ring and waits for me there, perfect posture, balled-up fists ready for a bareknuckle fight.

"I'm not going to fight you."

"Course not," Spencer chuckles, "you are too busy fighting yourself."

## FUCK YOU

The anger, he knows how to draw it out in long streaks of blood. It drips down the side of my still-raw, bruised face. I wipe it away, the blood drawn from punctured tongue.

I walk up to the middle of the ring.

Standing up straight, I stare him down.

Right before the first jab hits me in the left eye, he tells me, "You are only confused because you aren't willing to accept what waits for you. Everything that happens is a joke, a big fucking joke that's funny to no one but you. Why don't you laugh? Why don't you laugh, Sugar? Let loose and laugh. You are wound-up too tight! You can't hold onto the spotlight forever!"

## THAT'S WHAT YOU THINK

I look over at X, a set of eyes watching.

He throws a punch. I take it in stride.

"Why don't you laugh?"

Another punch to the face.

"I'm laughing!"

## JAB
## LEFT HOOK
## LEFT HOOK
## JAB

I stand there, arms crossed behind my back.

Spencer reopens wounds, worsens the numbness of this battle-torn body, but I might as well feel nothing. The placebos I take are enough to trick my manic mind into thinking that I'm not feeling anything at all.

"Why don't you laugh?"

## UPPERCUT

That one almost severs my tongue, teeth digging in deep, the stitches coming loose. Mild annoyance—

I will have to return to the hospital after this.
"Huh? Why don't you find this funny?"
Spencer punches me in the shoulder by accident.
This is where I would laugh.

## I DON'T FIND IT FUNNY

He shakes his hand, wincing in pain. Checks his knuckles.
They aren't boxer's knuckles.
"You don't find this funny, huh?"
This is the truth:

## NO

"I don't."
Spencer balls up his fists, back into a fighting stance, as he sends a combination:

## JAB
## JAB
## LEFT HOOK TO THE BODY
## RIGHT HOOK TO THE FACE

I cough, can't help it. The blood collects in my mouth from the torn gums and torn tongue.
"It's only funny when you fight yourself!"
Spencer shouts and I dodge the haymaker he aims right for the temple.
I push him back to the canvas.
Fists clenched, I stand there, bloody and out of breath:
He looks up at me, upset, "What are you waiting for?!"
But I don't. I refuse to fight a friend.
Back to his feet, he launches into a succession of jabs and hooks.
He beats it out of me, the truth.
He gets me to admit it.
Spencer shouts:

## WHY?!

"I don't trust you."

That last one really hurt.

After I say it as sincerely as I can, Spencer drops his fists, steps out of the ring and marches up the staircase.

Right before leaving my sight he pokes his head back down into view and says, "Everything that happens is part of the story you've written to be the person you want to be. I used to believe that it was just a fiction, a part of the identity you want to preserve. Now…I'm not so sure. Maybe you think they are switching places with you. No…they are all the same. You are all the same. Beating the ever-loving-shit out of yourself expecting something grand out of the finale. Here's your finale. Well here it is. Your finale! Can't see it?"

I look around the basement, unsure of what he's talking about.

"That's what I thought."

I hear laughter until it is muted by the closing of the basement door.

## SILENCE, NEAR SILENCE

The house creaks and moans to the mood of sheer confusion.

I look over at X.

"The fuck you looking at?"

He shuts his eyes, an indication of fear.

What must this look like to him? Am I really fighting someone other than myself?

I hear Spencer walking around upstairs and something about the pace of his footsteps upsets me. I pull up a chair to the TV in the corner of the basement. I turn it on and turn up the volume loud, anything to tune out what I hear, what seems to only be augmented in my mind.

The media has picked up on Executioner's disappearance.

I flip channels, turning it up louder as I look over my shoulder at X.

## YOU HEARING THIS?

Of course he is.

I relay what I see onscreen.

"Seems they are all concerned that you have been killed!"

## LOOK IN HIS DIRECTION

"Oh don't be that way, that's just one channel."

I see the formulas, how the media picks up a lead and lets it build, mounting until it sprouts the perfect version, the one that can be sensationalized to the fullest possible financial recompense.

"Here's another—seems they think that you cheated. I wonder where they heard that?"

## YEAH
## I WONDER...

"They think that you are exerting media silence. Good one."

I flip to yet another channel, "Seems the league officials are vacating the title since you've been unresponsive for more then seventy-two hours. Hmm. Well that's interesting. So Spencer got around to nabbing you days ago? What was he doing with you while I was bedridden in the hospital? Kissing your ass?"

Next channel—

I look over my shoulder, just to check to see if he's listening.

He's looking therefore I assume he's listening.

I just want to say something:

I think I'm a nice guy. If I sound like a bastard, it's because of what I'm going through right now. It's my mood. That's all. It's easy to treat X like a peon because I hate the man. He's everything I was and will probably go on to make better choices than I did.

Wow, that really does sound bad.

It makes me look like a douchebag.

But I didn't kidnap X. Spencer did.

His own choice.

## NOT MY FAULT

Even if he says that he's only doing what I told him to do or whatever.

I didn't tell him to take it too far. He operated on an assumption. Now, by the way the media is beginning to turn X into another case of title-dodging, it looks like everything is steamrolling forward.

One moment I want to take credit for the kidnapping.

Next moment I want to get the hell away from this.

Moment after next I worry about how the media portrays the disappearance; they don't have much of an imagination.

A series of moments, an aftermath, I forget all of the above and I am still flipping channels, collecting details about the disappearance.

I hear laughter.

For a long time, I fail to comprehend that the laughter that annoys is the laughter coming from me.

Those words quoted on television are mine.

The laughter that annoys is also the laughter that I love.

I look over my shoulder, and I say to X:

## YOU DON'T TRUST ME, DO YOU?

# THE LAUGHTER I LANGUISH

Vacated title means there's a whole lot of politics between all sorts of imperfect parties seeking the top contenders, the fighters that'll generate the most profit and attention for both league and all those invested. Vacated title means another fight. Vacated title means I am in the running but who knows if I'm the best I can be. Someone else is sure enough to be a better fit.

And yet my name ends up on the card alongside 'Black Mamba,' who didn't seem to exist until it appeared that I needed another challenge.

*Willem Floures vies for the title he held for over a decade.*
*Willem Floures faces his toughest opponent yet.*

## HIMSELF

And by that I mean, I'm not quite sure about my corner. I can pay for a cutman and all the other crewmembers, no problem, but there's the issue with Spencer, how he refuses to be in the same room as me. If I walk into a room, he is on his way out; if I need to speak to him, I only get my messages, my texts, my words, repeated back to me.

It seems I have to go at everything alone.

It seems I can, I will, I have already begun.

## I CAN SEE YOU FROM WHERE I'M SITTING

That's the first text message I get from what I hoped would be just another anonymous hater or fan—there tends to be one or two as long as you are worth talking about—but I quickly found out that the fight for the vacated title had already begun and Black Mamba got the first attack.

I text back, "Who is this?" like an idiot.
I know who it is.

## YES, LIKE AN IDIOT

And then a phone call which I ignore, not recognizing the number, but I listen to the voicemail moments after the prompt reads:

## ONE MISSED CALL
## NEW VOICEMAIL

Black Mamba calmly stating, "Hello, Willem. It's Willem. Been awhile hasn't it? It's getting a bit weird, hmm? Seems you can't help but step on your own toes, retracing your steps from one event to the next. What was the deal with the tattoos? Aren't you too old for body modification?" There's a pause and then, "Anyway, I'm always just around the corner. Don't you make too many mistakes. We have to make this fight interesting."

End of message. End of common sense.

Questionable if I ever had any.

After listening to the voicemail for a second time, I wander into the basement bathroom. I look at my face, "This is my face, I guess."

I check my arms, "What does he mean by 'modification?'"

I take off my shirt and I discover designer scarring combined with a multiple color tattoo wrapping around my chest and back. When did I get this?

But I guess even Black Mamba is unsure.

## THAT'S ODD

Shirt back on, noticing that the tattoo isn't sore, it has healed over, the scarring looks to have been something done long enough ago to be complete. The scarring, I can't imagine when I could have gotten the work done.

Hasn't it only been a few days?

## IT HAS BEEN A FEW MONTHS

It has? Who said that?

## IT'S WILLEM. YOU ARE READING
## TEXT MESSAGES RECEIVED

I look around the basement. I see that X isn't looking well. I wander over to him and notice that although he looks malnourished, someone has been cleaning him. There is no smell. New clothes, the chaffing against wrist and ankle have been treated. Executioner is being slowly executed, tortured by deprivation of food and nutrition.

I mutter, "But even he isn't alone…"

There are three more of me, tied up, taped up, and watching, judging, worrying about what will become of me. They all have nametags:

We already know about X.

## WHO ARE THE OTHERS?

That's what I want to know.

'Rattlesnake.'

'Breakneck.'

'Big Boy.'

With everyone tied up and left side by side, the sight of them hurts my head. I get dizzy, the kind of reaction and altered vision that comes from a particularly bad concussion.

## A "BEAT UP THE CHAMPION" MEDIA EVENT
## WILL DO THAT

I'm again searching for not only a response but also a reason. What the hell happened? No answer. But I check for any soreness; I find a particularly alarming bump on the right side of my head. With a single touch, I feel something that is probably pain.

I get another phone call.

Mamba.

For some reason I pick it up. When he speaks to me it's like he's a voice in my head, "Don't be an idiot. You can feel pain. I'm going to make sure you never feel one hundred percent again. This fight will be your last!"

He hangs up but I keep talking into the phone, not letting the call end:

"What the hell are you talking about? When did this happen? When is the fight? Wait, what?"

Read into the fact that I am talking into the receiver long after the call has ended. I am not talking to anyone.

## YOU ARE TALKING TO ME

"Wait, what?" I look over at them as if they'll be able to explain what's going on to me, all taped up, starving, parts of me dying slowly.

How much of me is dead?

How long does it take for someone to completely die inside?

## EVERYTHING YOU SAY, I HEAR
## EVERYTHING I HEAR, YOU DREAD

*What to not read into:* I am not afraid.

## THAT CHARITY EVENT DIDN'T GO SO WELL

Suddenly feeling a surge of anxiety, I punch one of them in the face as hard as I can. My knuckles crack upon impact.

*What to not read into:* I am not in pain.

I shout his name, "Spencer!"

I can sense that he heard me from upstairs.

Laughter. I do a double take, listening for the source. It isn't me. It isn't them. I silently wander the perimeter of the ring, until I see that someone has left their phone, it's playing out a video sequence where I am front-and-center, talking to a large crowd like I'm confident.

Like I don't have issues with public speaking.

Like I am on my own, no Spencer to be seen.

Like I'm not worrying about that, about the fact that Spencer can't be seen in either media and my memory. What is he up to?

I can't answer that question until I've figured out what I've been doing.

## YOU KIND OF COME OFF AS A FOOL IN THIS INTERVIEW

## WHAT WERE YOU THINKING?

I pause the video, I replay the part where I threaten a celebrity I've never met. What was I thinking?

"You talentless hack! If I could fight any celebrity in the ring, it would be you!" Again with the laughter.

That is at my expense. It is always at my expense.

Pause. Rewind. Replay.

It seems I'm late to every realization.

## THE FIGHT IS IN TWO DAYS

I try to call the number.

The phone pauses the video and reads:

Incoming call, Loser.

Vacated title means a vacated venture where I'm the slowest reader of them all. Happenstance is intentional and Black Mamba's threats hit real close.

"Spencer! Where did these guys come from?"

They watch me. They are all younger than me.

Have been training, it seems; they have the make and conditioning of a primetime fighter. Boxing the best, a bunch of Willems.

I tell them, "This is your future," while holding a handful of flab from my stomach, pinching it to the point where it feels like one of those foam tubes used as floatation devices in swimming pools.

## NICE ONE

Attached to the text message is a picture I've seen before but for some reason don't remember. It is a screen-cap of an online article discussing a certain sort of madness, yet again at my expense.

The author apparently spoke to me about my career and I proceed to act so humble and selfless, praising every single accomplishment that can't be linked to 'Sugar.' I talk about how I intend on a few more fights but retirement is likely a possibility.

I talk about being an organ donor.

I talk about a few charities.

The article reads well except for when I make a racist comment towards the end, the screen-cap image being a zoom in of the exact line; it went viral, spread like wildfire across social media.

It seems I missed another call.

It's...you know who it is.

"Willem, you really know how to get their attention. You take whatever you can get. Bad publicity still gets you places."

End of message.

I delete it only to see that I have a number of saved messages.

Different numbers, that all too familiar voice.

*What to not read into:* I am not confused.

## LEAVE THE COMEDY FOR THE PROFESSIONALS

Black Mamba with a bunch of bad jokes, really bad ones, apparently from a comedy routine I tried at an open mic/improv event. I comb through my memory but cannot seem to find a thread that pulls in the right direction, the one where I realize that I've been doing all of this.

Combing through, I come up empty-handed.

Each voicemail is more alarming than the last.

I wonder if I knew what I was doing the moment I mentioned something about murder.

## YOU KILLED A MAN?

Apparently. I remember that.

I also remember there being four of them, not six.

X, Rattlesnake, Breakneck, and Big Boy.

'Earthquake' and 'Q-Bert' are unfamiliar.
*What not to read into:* I am worried.
Worried about what?
Exactly.

## FOCUS ON THE UPCOMING FIGHT

I keep forgetting that the title is vacated. Anyone can be Willem Floures and everyone that wants to be me has been tied up and kidnapped by Spencer, brought down to this basement.

This used to be where I trained, now it's more of a prison.

And yet I can't really leave, can I?

I still feel safe here, safer than upstairs where the hauntings seem to be two steps ahead. The house still shifts and groans with every anxiety.

I keep getting the feeling that I'm being watched.

"Spencer?"

I'll have to leave the basement at some point; might as well see what's going on today. It is odd to find out that it's dark outside. It feels like I've been awake for only a few moments. I listen to the house for the sound of footsteps, a very specific sort of creaking, like the sound of someone falling over, croaking, after landing a power shot right to the stomach.

Mouth guard falling out.

I follow the sound of would-be footsteps, only finding out later that they are mine. My footsteps take me on a tour of the house, as if I'm trying to show myself that I'm alone.

I get it. I'm alone.

## WHO ARE YOU GOING TO HAVE IN YOUR CORNER ON FIGHT NIGHT?

I tune that out.

*What not to read into:* The fact that I am all of these things and yet uncertain of much of anything.

The neurosis of the past couple months (days? How long has it been?) keeps things inconsistent but then again when is life really at balance?

Yes, there are worries.

Yes, there are fears.

Yes, there are omissions from memory.

And yes, there seems to be a lot lacking in that particular category. Memory. But it's mostly understood. I know that they are in here, in this skull of mine…when I see the evidence, it is more like remembering than having never seen it before. I seem to be passed over, the world and it's all-too-important media getting ahead of me.

I'm the one running, gassed, left gasping for breath.

## DO YOU REMEMBER WHEN YOU PULLED THAT TOOTH OUT ON LIVE TV AND WERE SUBSEQUENTLY BANNED FROM THE SHOW?

When I read this text message, I can sense that it's happened. My tongue, now healed over (as if only noticing now), instinctively goes to the right tooth, the tooth now clearly a fake, an expensive replacement.

I wouldn't have noticed if I hadn't known of it before.

Yeah, but then I still have the same inquiries of self-loathing.

The whole, "What were you thinking?" pangs of regret that quickly send me into shame spirals.

Like right now, I realize that I'm aimlessly walking the entirety of the house, not really paying attention to anything (not that there's anything to notice; the house is empty); I might have noticed that Sarah's room is unlocked. I might have noticed that Sarah isn't home. No sign of Spencer. The hauntings that brew in these spaces are never near enough, close enough of a connection, for an encounter. Not like James or whatever is going to say hello.

I don't sense a disturbance.

I only hear Black Mamba's voice, commenting on everything I do.

## YOU ARE THREATENING ME

And of course that's not me saying those things. Black Mamba parlays threat with accusation of a threat.

Recognize that everything in my life is a fight that might not ever be fully won. Read into the fact that there are less factual elements and more of an identity exaggerated and sensationalized, controlled and destroyed, contradicted and rendered inconsistent, for the sake of the media's interest.

I am unreliable.

I am unforgivable. I am in denial…

All for the sake of the identity I've conceived.

Sell a little to gain a lot. Or whatever.

## I AM GOING TO KNOCK YOU OUT BY RD FIVE

This is all part of pre-fight psychology. There's the tendency for your opponent to attempt to derail your focus, your ability to concentrate on fight strategy, but when you are fighting yourself, the psychology is yours to over-analyze and let consume via an obsession.

There are too many layers to the fight.

I can't go at the fight alone.

"Spencer…?"

I hear his voice but it's drowned out by Black Mamba's.

"Spencer…? I can't hear you. Speak up!"

## HE'S TRYING TO TELL YOU THE TRUTH

I know the truth.

Shut up! I can't figure out where he is.

## HE'S IN YOUR CORNER, TRYING TO TELL YOU WHAT YOU NEED TO DO TO WIN

What I need to win? I need to win, that's all I need to know. I need to keep my sights on the victory. The big "v." I can't let you get to me. I can't lose. If you win, I will have lost myself. I might as well be a person dead on their feet, lost in his own grey matter, a thread of half-thoughts and haywire actions.

Willem Floures:

One of those celebrity athlete personalities that took a turn for the worse. People claiming "he's manic depressive" and "he's out of control."

Read into what I don't want to read into:

Fear.

Worry.

Fear and worry that it is all real.

Not imagined.

My fight record is ruined.

I used to be the best of the best.

And that's not an egotistical statement, okay?

## BUT YOU AREN'T LISTENING

I can't help but listen.

Maybe it's you that doesn't want to listen.

*You* can get out of my headspace. I can't.

I can't escape.

I have nowhere else to go but back in the basement. I need to train. Two days until fight night. I need to train.

## USELESS, YOU NEVER TRAIN, YOU DON'T READ INTO THE RHYTHM SURROUNDING YOUR LIFE

Believe me, I tried.

Past tense, I know. I "try." Better? But I don't want to read into this, any of what's already happened. Publicity is publicity. I am right there, in the spotlight. I am still the WILLEM FLOURES.

There is a whole lot of fight left in me.

Look—

I mean see all of them?

There were six, now there are eight.

That's a number that delves right into my losses. Each and every one of them is a potential defeat that can't happen if I don't let them go. I tie them up; I pretend that they don't exist. Somehow Spencer continues to find them and bind them. I won't question it.

I still don't like the idea of kidnapping the competition, but then again, I don't know what I like and dislike.

Really it can only end up hurting me in the end.

## THEN WHY LET IT HAPPEN?

It seems everything is already happening with or without me!

I'm the last person to know and I'm the one that's at the very center of every scuffle, every media-drenched accusation, every dreaded flicker, flash of the camera.

I don't have a whole lot of time to read into things.

I have lost any structure to the identity I continue to destroy (define?).

No time to fight the thoughts; I will have to fight myself in the ring, to a sold-out arena, in two days.

I need to train.

## EVERYTHING YOU READ IS TRUE

That might be true but I can't let this brand of laughter languish. It's laughter that is at my expense. It is laughter that should motivate me. I should focus and keep to the search within.

I realize that it sounds stupid but there has to be a reason why I want to be the best, right?

I want your attention, their attention.

I want you to realize that I can beat you.

## YOU WON'T BEAT ME

I will beat you.

## IF YOU BEAT ME, YOU END UP LOSING TO YOURSELF

Don't start with that. It has no effect on me.

I have long since lost interest in the subject. How we even exist is a matter of subjectivity. Looks like anyone that isn't in the spotlight is cast in a brand of doubt. In fact, if there's no brand there's no brain, nobody there.

It makes sense that Willem Floures is a popular brand.

Everyone wants to be me.

I have to keep fighting if I don't want things to change.

THEY CHANGE
EVERY MOMENT THEY CHANGE
LOOK WHERE YOU ARE NOW
VERSUS WHERE YOU WERE
LOOK HOW IN TWO DAYS YOU WILL BE
BEDRIDDEN AND FORCIBLY RETIRED

I choose not to read the last text message. I suddenly feel overwhelmed. I get in the ring, I take off my shirt and shoes, I look down at the design so permanent; I trace the ridge of one scar, a circular border around a purple and green dragon tattoo. I consciously tune out what I hear as well as the impossibilities that are now, somehow, in progress.

I tell them all, noticing that they are all watching me, "Life doesn't make sense. If it does, maybe you're dead."

I consciously keep things simple.

I don't read into any more of it. No not at all. I start shuffling around the ring, warming up my legs, practicing footwork.

I begin shadowboxing.

Clear-headed, phone set aside, Black Mamba is of no issue. The only issue is figuring out what training routines to stress in the next forty-eight hours.

What is most effective?

What will have any real effect?

Really though, how long can my mind remain clear before the inconsistencies you see and read so clearly resurface as yet another washed-out wave of apprehension? Am I getting too old for this?

*Please, don't read into*: The fact that my mind is misaligned, getting cloudy with confusion and self-conflict…how long did I last?

A dozen punches, a series of jabs.

Two minutes before the latest chapter collapses and your

identity is further fraught with internal conflict, fright, worry, loathing, contradiction, hypocritical undertones, worry again, repeat, repeat, bad memory, problems, life is meaningless, alone, fight in two days, worry, anxiety, need to train, Spencer where are you, Sarah too, existential questions and—end this train of thought *now*.

# THE LAUGHTER I ALIGN

*But my train of thought continues*—with laughter, laughter, worry that ____ is a result of ____ and a history of fighting results in a broken mind, laughter at me, a joke, I'm a joke, laughter at fact that I think any of this training is going to help, laughter at fact that I made a fool of myself to remain in the spotlight, laughter at fact that I can't remember any of it, laughter at fact that I am still somehow proud of it, laughter at the enjoyment I get from being a "relevant subject," laughter I hear whenever thinking about legacy, will I be remembered, will Willem Floures be as good of a boxing commodity when I'm done, laughter heard when I think about all that I've done to be noteworthy, laughter and then debase myself, laughter upon laughter when dealing with all aspects of this, what?, laughter, what?, laughter abounds when, yet again, everything is confused and I don't know what the hell I'm doing much less what I was thinking about right before it all faded, lost train of thought. End train of thought.

Continue training, despite myself.

## I DON'T KNOW WHO I AM ANYMORE

Okay, duly noted. But there's a fight tomorrow.

I must do something, must focus on something productive, something that helps buffer the incoming events, the events that *haven't* already transpired and been lost to a poor memory.

## DID YOU HEAR SOMETHING?

I'd ask them but they know as much as I do. Their mouths are taped shut. Their minds are broken apart. Their routines shattered; all they can do is watch. All they have left is their sight and what they see is their future.

Maybe they think they can do better, become a much better fighter, and that might be true but I will tell them that no matter what happens, we are viewed to be the same person more often than we are viewed as ourselves.

## THE FIGHT

I know, I know.

The fight is tomorrow.

## THE FIGHT IS TONIGHT

It is not tonight.

Wait a minute…

Black Mamba leaves another voicemail. I don't have to listen to it to know that he sent me a sample of the press conference where he said something that I capitalized upon much to the appreciation (and delight) of everyone but myself.

I turn to them and say, "I came out of the press conference on the up. Black Mamba really walked into that one huh?"

No replies.

But they know.

I'm the last to realize what happened.

## WHAT HAPPENED, 'SUGAR?'

I want to text back, "Don't patronize me," but that'll just open up another avenue of communication. I refuse to let Black Mamba continue sabotaging my state of mind. If the fight is really tonight, I need to focus.

Shit, I need to train…

I ask the latest kidnapping, 'Hatchet,' if there's anything I can possibly do in the next four hours before I need to be on the way to the arena.

## WHY ARE YOU ASKING HIM?

Black Mamba, get out of my mind! Focus on the fight. Let me go about this the only way I know: an introspective and interpretive, but ultimately long-winded, exploration of who, what, when, where, and how.

The five questions.

The five senses.

Number of rounds covered to a twelve round fight where I come up two rounds short. The last two are the toughest and I often leave nothing left for those twilight hours, those miserable last gasps.

I never think about the future.

I'm consistently stuck in the present.

## DID YOU HEAR SOMETHING?

Easy enough to ignore the threats, the mind play, when I have such a great and receptive audience!

"How many of you are there, hmm?"

I count sixteen but what happens if I look away?

Will I see Spencer dragging another one in?

How many people really desire to be someone preexisting?

"I am Willem Floures!" I shout at the lineup.

Turning around, I meet the seventeenth, "And let me guess, you are…"

Willem Floures.

'Lights Out' Willem Floures.

"Hey Lights Out, what's your fight record," I untie all tethers but the ones binding his wrists together. He doesn't need to say anything; he's going to be my sparring opponent. We are going to have one last bit of training before I face Black Mamba. And about his fight record, I can only assume that he's undefeated; I am undefeated at such a young age. It's basically a prerequisite.

Everything is easy, anxious, and hopeful when you are young.

It's only when you've climbed every rung of the ladder that you see that they've all been following you too, every damn version.

So what do you do?

You confuse them; you confuse yourself.

Confusion, contradiction, complete chaos seems to be the only means of keeping me in the spotlight.

I set up a twelve round sparring session.

We'll take it slow. I only need someone to evade.

## DID YOU HEAR SOMETHING?

I hear the TV and I hear my phone but I don't hear you.

## YOUR FLIGHT LEAVES IN TWO HOURS

Round one, I work on my footwork. Lights Out makes it easy, sprinting towards the ropes, making no attempt at facing me.

It's my duty to keep him from climbing out of the ring.

He keeps me on the balls of my feet, strafing with my fists up, covering my face just in case he tries lunging at me.

I know enough about how I fight in the ring.

If it were I, I'd kick and squirm. I would try to land a head-butt right where it hurts most. However, for the majority of the round, Lights Out has no trouble reaching the ropes but by the time I get to him, he is an easy and effortless push back into the middle of the ring.

I see tears streaming down his face.

I tell him, "Hey now, calm yourself. This is only round one."

## DO YOU HEAR SOMETHING?

Round two I decide to work on my left-right-right jab combination. It isn't a specialty but I have always had trouble switching up jabs. It's too predictable jabbing with the same hand. Spencer always said that it pays to switch stances if you are the type of fighter that can switch from right to left and back.

I hide my southpaw stance for as long as I can—not because they don't know that I'm a leftie but because it is frustrating to note that your opponent is still holding something back. But even trying to be unpredictable becomes predictable and with

Black Mamba swimming around in my head, I'm going to try all sorts of strategies. I'm going to explore what it means to not make any sense. Black Mamba, You know what I hear?

I hear everyone laughing at you.

I hear that not all is what it seems.

## THEY LOVED YOU AT THE HEIGHTS

Round three is all about continuing to practice the jab.

My mind circles around a thought bubble that has yet to burst. I want to know what it is but there is little more than the mental residue of sensation and the name 'Nicole.' The Heights.

I land a succession of jabs, watching Lights Out shut his eyes, bracing for impact. I work the stomach rather than merely going for the chin.

This is a sparring session. I don't intend on going full-force, using whatever's left in the tank.

The Heights. Half of the round passes before the bubble bursts and the details come crashing out. The Heights—a celebrity dinner party for cancer prevention. Black Mamba made an appearance. I made the party. It seems I delivered a speech that brought tears to their eyes and a smile to their faces.

What the hell was I thinking?

Well whatever it was, I did well.

I got their attention.

Proof that I can be peaceful as long as it's about publicity.

## THEY LOVED YOU AT ONLOCATION

During round four, Lights Out's legs begin to buckle. I have to lift him up; he won't (or maybe he can't) stand up on his own feet. I threaten him to cooperate, "This is about winning the title!"

His eyes roll back into his skull.

I slap him across the face, "Don't you realize how important this is for us?" By round five I'm propping him up, shouting into his face, "At this rate, you'll never be me!" The round is a throwaway unless clinching is a worthy enough strategy (it isn't—not for this fight).

By round six, I have to put Lights Out back with the rest.

"At least there are more of you. More the merrier, it seems.

"Hey X, want to redeem yourself? How about a couple rounds of sparring?" His eyes are closed.

"No…?"

Hear the uncertainty in my voice? That's because I haven't a clue where this is going, the kidnappings.

I shadowbox for the duration of the round.

Occasionally I stop to ask them questions about myself:

"Do I like chocolate?"

"Am I considered to be more of a dirty blonde or brown-haired man?"

"That last fight, it really didn't look like it was me, huh?"

"That last fight felt like I was an imposter, right?"

I know…

It's true.

"Imposter…"

"Which one of you is an imposter?"

"Am I the imposter?"

## YOU ARE THE IMPOSTER

Shut the fuck up.

"Are you guys hearing this?"

"You know, Black Mamba? He's in my damn head. I can hear him saying what he texts me."

"You aren't hearing this?"

## THEY LOVED YOU AT GRETCHEN LIVE

"Everybody, what the hell is 'Gretchen Live?'

"A daytime talk show?

"I don't know what it is."

Some of them stare. Some of them are barely there.

Some of them watch and nod.

One of them, Breakneck, looks like he's given up the ghost, neck craned back at an impossible angle, skin like porcelain.

Yeah, he's probably towards the end of his run. I would say it's a shame but I don't really know what's more shameful—the fact that he died while tied down or the fact that there are over eighteen of me more or less populating the basement.

The latter is likely to be the more shameful of the two.

"Gretchen Live, anyone?"

"X, you?"

I wish I could sleep away the next few days. Give it enough time and the memory unveils itself. How much would I relive in my dreams?

"Do I remember my dreams?

"Huh?

"What about this Gretchen Live thing? Anyone?"

## I JUST TRIED TO CALL YOU

I check my phone, new voicemail. Fine, I'll listen.

"Hey, it's *Willem*..."

I brace for humiliation only to discover that I was the talk of the town. Gretchen loved what I had to say. I spoke intellectually about topics I don't know anything about. I am able to hold a conversation with a prestigious daytime talk-show host and philanthropist.

I am a highlight for the day.

Other media venues recap what I said on Gretchen Live.

One quote is, "He's poignant. Who would have thought—a pugilist that's poignant?"

Return to my audience.

"How's that for awesome and unexpected?"

What I'm looking for here is a laugh, a round of applause, but okay they aren't in the mood and really I can't expect them to share my enthusiasm.

This has everything to do with us but, somehow, at the same time, it is exclusively mine. Hey Black Mamba, worried that I've stolen of the spotlight?

Nothing.

No text, no reply.

Thought so.

What now?
Round seven.

## THEY LOVED YOU AT SPARE CHANGE

*Oh fucking hell.*
"Do any of you know if I have a temper?"

I feel like I should have a temper; theoretically, a fighter can snap into sudden anger for almost no reason and people would forgive it. They'll say something like:

He's a fighter. Fighters are brimming with adrenaline and negative charge. It would stereotypically make sense that I lose my temper.

"Right?

"Anyone know if I know what I'm talking about?

"X? Of course not."

Sometimes I do.

I feel momentary lapses of confidence and assurance, like right at this very moment, only to fall back into a semi-confused state.

I'm way too lost in my head, I think.

"I just want to make sure, do I have blue or brown eyes?"

"When I throw one of my signature left hooks," I throw a few, letting the last one hit the ropes, "do they look like they'd hurt?

"Well, do they?"

## YOUR EYES ARE JET BLACK

They are brown, I assure you.

## JET BLACK, LIKE THE SADDEST NIGHT

I ignore Black Mamba. I assert myself as *the* Willem Floures by walking up to the turnbuckle, climbing it and, from where I am, I look down at all of them, the number now being…

Via another head count:

Twenty-five.

I ask them, "Why are you Willem Floures?

"Why must you be the best Willem can be?

"Why do we beat the sense out of ourselves fight after fight?"
Round seven is a battle of the mind.

*Disclaimer:* I need to define each round in order to be able to direct myself through every action without losing something in the process.

It's not unlike the impulse every single self-respecting individual has to continually redefine who he or she is with every single pulse.

"Who am I right now?

"How about now?

"And now?"

I flex my biceps, mock victory pose.

I might not see the boundaries; I may not be able to answer the questions I've posed, but at this moment, I feel good, confident, about as courageous as I currently look, standing on the second turnbuckle, victory pose like the best of the best.

"Can I really go another twelve rounds?"

## DON'T WORRY
## IT WON'T TAKE THAT LONG

"Well who got the last laugh at Spare Change?!"

That is directed to Black Mamba, who I bet won't reply. I listen in, expecting to hear crickets, nothing if not because he is a one-sided predator, capable only of loose threats and complete carnage. His only card is that of the enigma, the young, boastful boxer poised to induce an upset.

Victory will not be yours.

## DID YOU HEAR SOMETHING?

I shout, as if he's in the basement with me, "Don't avoid the fucking question, Mamba!"

## SEEMS I ALREADY ANSWERED YOUR QUESTION

"No you didn't!"

## THE PHONE

The voicemail. I drop down from the turnbuckle. I grab my phone resting on the tabletop, right next to the TV, and I listen.

"Hello, it's *Willem*—"

Just like him to start the message with a patronizing "hello." He goes on and on about altruism and how it's great that I'm such a kindhearted celebrity. But when he mentions the true punk-anarchist nature of Spare Change, how it vouches and promotes public cacophony via vandalization, rebellious artistic expression, how it basically aims to support what I denied at the Heights, I begin to lose that edge. Confidence slips away from me as I begin to sweat.

End of message.

*To repeat this message—*

## DID YOU HEAR SOMETHING?

I look at them half expecting one of them to break free of the harnesses. I take a step towards the turnbuckle. I see them wince.

I shake my head, disappointed.

Suddenly dejected, the enthusiasm, the confident charge of my sparring session depleted by yet another notice of my mania.

My hypocritical fight for the full spotlight.

"But anyone would do the same, right?"

Yeah, no answer.

## DID YOU HEAR SOMETHING?

"What?! What am I supposed to be hearing?"

I hop up onto the top turnbuckle, reaching towards the ceiling.

"I'm listening, Mamba."

## IMAGINE WHAT THIS MUST LOOK LIKE

"I'm fine. I don't know what you're talking about."

## YOU ARE NOT FINE
## YOU ARE TALKING TO YOURSELF

"What if I told you I was talking to Spencer?"

## HOW COULD YOU BE?
## HE'S ALREADY THERE
## WAITING FOR YOU AT THE VENUE
## WHAT IF I TOLD YOU 'EXECUTIONER' SHOULD
## HAVE NEVER EVEN FOUGHT IN THE FIRST PLACE?
## WHERE WOULD YOU BE NOW? WOULD YOU STILL
## BE FIGHTING ME?

I am, as always, the last to know.

*Disclaimer:* My mind is ripe with mania.

Between what I do to remain relevant and what I do to remain myself, there is no middle, no sense to the nonsense.

Nonsense is pure publicity.

Nonsense is what ultimately keeps me as a cultural commodity.

A fighter must fight all aspects of himself if he wants to win the fight.

*And the world's favor.*

"I spent a lifetime winning their favor; you aren't taking it from me now!"

*Disclaimer:* I am sure that I'm not talking to myself.

## DISCLAIMER:
## YOU ARE GOING TO BE LATE TO THE FIGHT

I look at my captive audience.

They look at me.

We know at the very same time what happens next.

I fall from the turnbuckle, nearly twisting my ankle.

I curse Black Mamba's name, which means I curse my own name, our name, whatever...

I crawl over to the ropes, pulling myself back up to my feet.

I limp up the stairs shouting, "A win without a fight is not a win!"

## THERE WILL BE A FIGHT

## I'LL HOLD THE FIRST TWO ROUNDS AGAINST YOU

## BETTER HOPE YOU GOT SOMETHING MORE THAN IDENTITY ANOMIE

*Disclaimer:* I am not going to apologize.

The nonsense forms its own sort of identity.

In a world where everything is worth only a moment's notice, I care most about the favor and the future of Willem Floures.

It might sound indulgent but it's true:

*We all fight to be recognized.*

My ability to understand who I am has been slaughtered, the gore and blood smeared across national media. Every single article, be it a picture or a long blog post, an article for the Times or a video interview uploaded, I say what I say and I deny it in the next. I say one thing only to sever any understanding with a follow-up series of episodes.

The media thinks it's all an act.

The media thinks of me as a nutcase. But they like enigmatic undertones; they love an eccentric personality.

They'd take tumor minds over yet another brandless tool.

And you know what?

I'll take it.

I'll take whatever I can get.

## DID YOU HEAR SOMETHING?

I sigh, "Just tell me."

## YOU ALREADY KNOW

A moment later I did. I should be happy, thrilled.

It was going to happen.

*Everything I had aligned made true.*

Maybe I didn't have it all figured out.

Maybe it wasn't supposed to be this way.

But it was going to happen. Despite what it took to get there, for a brief moment, I would take the spotlight.

One last time.

# VERSUS

Maybe you don't trust me. I don't trust me. Okay, fine. You don't trust me. Well at least trust in the fact that I have this fight won. I am as prepared as I could ever be. Black Mamba hasn't a clue what I'll use, how I'll fight, or how this will go down. It's why he keeps asking me if I hear something.

I hear all.

So let's stick to the basics, okay?

I want to explain something to you; I want to talk about the basics of the perfect boxing match. What can and will go wrong versus what can and will go right: the anatomy of a twelve round fight for the title.

So let's have at it, but keep in mind that I didn't get to the arena in time. Rounds one and two were withheld, via judge bribery, the match wasn't thrown out but the first two rounds were certainly given to Mamba.

Foolish of me to think that it was Spencer that paid off the judges. Never would have thought it was Black Mamba's camp that made it so.

But I guess they need this fight to happen.

They want the fight because they want the spotlight.

Spencer, he sits in the corner barking orders that don't make any sense. And I mean that literally—

He shouts incoherent commands, a great frown on his face, followed by the only thing I can make out:

ARE YOU LISTENING?

I guess not. But I got this covered. Again, this is about trust. Trust me more than I can trust myself.

Who else am I going to trust? I can't trust Spencer, who

systematically unwrites the entire league by capturing every single potential fighter before they've reached their fifteenth fight. I can't trust someone I trusted for almost two decades. I can't... even begin to finish that sentence.

## TWO DECADES

More or less—all that time, my career being equally his career. I'm speechless just thinking about how much went into our professional relationship only to have this happen. He says I'm the one that's changed. Everyone changes as they age. I think he's changed for the worse.

I can't listen to his lectures anymore.

They go right over my head.

## ARE YOU LISTENING?

No I'm not but I hope you are.

Pay attention.

This one's going to be a barnburner.

## ROUND THREE

After a bit of crowd-pleasing via the ring announcer and one of the producers covering for my tardiness, I am in my corner and Black Mamba in his. Though he looks at me, I feel like he is looking through me. Looking past me. We walk to the center of the ring, touch gloves, and the bell sounds.

Immediately I notice something's wrong.

I can't place the problem, but it's there. The entire fight is off; the momentum isn't there.

At first I figure it's because Black Mamba is a counterpuncher. This is unexpected.

He waits for me to make a mistake and he counters with a combination, often trailing the light jabs and hooks with a shot that might just knock my head off. But they are few and far between.

For the duration of the round, I watch as Black Mamba

maintains a defensive shell.

I am trying to figure him out and, for these first few rounds, I give him the benefit of the doubt: He's probably doing the same.

Though I know what he's thinking, just as he knows what's swirling around in my head, between the physical and the mental there is a difference, an omission. I can surprise him with an instinctual strike or he might forego strategy and fight on pure adrenaline, feeling out the fight and nothing more.

That's the thing about boxing—

Though it is a science…

Though it requires skill and intellect to master…

The body often falls into its own pace, its own groove.

Everything you build snaps into effect and during the best moments of the round, you are seeing a flurry of images; you are acting and reacting without any trigger of the mind.

It's a lot like how time can pass so quickly when you are having a wonderful time; the round can pass by in a split second, leaving you reeling, catching images of various encounters. You can only hope you landed the most punches and the CompuBox has you on the up rather than down.

Plus, hopefully you aren't bleeding.

No cuts, that kind of thing.

End of the round, I feel like nothing's happened. Take it as another example of what I'm trying to explain.

During the best fights, I often feel like I am the one, the only Willem Floures. No shred of a doubt—I am who I've been and the reason I fight is because the fight keeps things simple and obvious.

Reason: You want to win.

Reason: You want to impress the world.

Reason: It makes you feel alive.

Reason: It's the only thing you're certain of—the fight involves not losing, winning to make everyone happy, and, last but not least, fighting is the truest testament to being alive.

If you aren't fighting, you are dying.

## ROUND FOUR

It passes in the blink of an eye.

I pretend to be frustrated, throwing lots of punches that don't connect, so that I can set myself up for a surprise in the following round.

Mamba remains on the defensive, wasting away the round with very little activity. Between rounds, Spencer is still going on and on about something, shouting as loud as he can possibly stomach. I clear my throat, take in some water, breathe in and out three times; one of the crewmembers checks my face, looking for any cutting.

The last thing I want is to feel the vapors of the Vaseline on my face, the Vaseline they rub into every cut to keep from further tearing and damage. That's reason enough to fight effectively:

Take no risks.

Know when to let go and know when to lead your opponent on.

And I'm not talking about first-date etiquette here.

## ARE YOU LISTENING?

Spencer shouts. I heard that last part.

Fine, yeah. I nod. Whatever you say.

## ROUND FIVE

I've encountered some of the younger ones trying to be a swarmer, thinking that the onslaught of punches and aggression will take me out, but remember what I said about my chin? I can take a punch. I can take a hundred punches and I'll remain standing. Maybe not now, but back in the day I could.

Now I maintain the illusion that I can.

Hell, maybe I can; I don't know.

Everything I've thought to be true has turned out to be false; everything I've thought to be false turns out to be true. There is no pattern and everything is a ploy trying to render me confused.

I've encountered one that wasted all his energy trying to knock me out with haymakers. He tried to bolo punch me into a situation where I'd fall into one of his power punches. Yeah right.

He lasted four fights before dropping the name.

Whoever he is now, he isn't Willem Floures.

I can't even recall his fight alias. What was it?

Black Mamba hides behind his fists. The thing about counterpunchers is they play conservatively but if you go southpaw and fight more like a swarmer, at least in small spurts, you will land a few punches. Even if he has a strong defense, he won't be able to avoid every punch. First thirty seconds into the round, I begin to notice that every time I land a punch Mamba buckles.

There's no way a single jab can hurt him.

I land a straight to the body and he buckles.

It's these kinds of things that worry me. The majority of this round consists of idle jabbing followed by analysis of Mamba's intentions.

I throw a succession of jabs, following it up with the clinch.

Spitting out my mouth guard, I whisper into his ear, "What the fuck are you doing? Fight!"

No response, not even a grimace or glare. Behind those lifeless eyes, I discover the fight to be a decoy, one that I can't help but accept.

I have to win even though the worry is placed elsewhere.

The rest of the round, neither of us is active.

I hear Spencer's hoarse voice in the background, disregarded commands from a once trusted source.

Even he couldn't tell me what's going on.

The fact that I know only makes this worse.

End of the round, back to the corner, the cutman rubs that Vaseline over my face, I spit into a bucket, take in deep breaths.

Spencer with commands, Spencer behaving as expected.

## ARE YOU LISTENING?

No, I'm not.

I am two steps ahead, post-fight, looking back at what I had told you would be my comeback, a great fight. A real back-to-basics.

I never expected to face myself in the ring.

I know that's a contradictory statement. I know, *I know*:

When have I not fought myself in the ring? The fight is an internal struggle. Yeah, all that philosophical stuff, but right over there, sitting on that stool, that thing staring back at me...

He's not alive.

There's no one there.

I can see right through Black Mamba. I see into the future.

I see into round nine when it happens.

I get my first knockout in quite a long time.

When the bell rings for round six, I can promise you one thing:

This fight will not go the distance.

## ROUND SIX

He stands there, gloves up, idle and unwilling to trade punches.

Who are you to think that I will let you throw the fight! Hear those words echo out through my head. I see through Black Mamba and I see the perfect publicity stunt.

They have fallen for it.

The entirety of round six we stand there in the center of the ring, not a single punch thrown and yet the audience falls for it.

They devour every round like the main-event it should be, not realizing what has been derailed.

I drop my hands.

I look up at the crowd, scanning up to the nosebleed section.

On their faces are grins, smiles, shocked and amused expressions; on their faces are the indications of one of the greatest fights of all time.

I lower my gaze to the ring.

Mamba remains shelled up, predictable fighting stance.

I return to my corner, the rest of the round wasted.

Spencer delivers the memorized speech, the one I ignore.

## ARE YOU LISTENING?

It is right then that I realize that it isn't Spencer that's asking me if I'm listening. It's Black Mamba. I see that he's still standing in the middle of the ring, his crew splashing water, Spencer his trainer, delivering similar lines, maybe the same lines, failing to notice that their fighter remains standing, waiting to beat himself up.

I hear the same garbled noises, the same use of Vaseline on nonexistent facial cuts, I notice the repetition of every minute detail, right before round seven begins. When it does, I watch the crowd, clearly aware that they aren't tuning into the same fight.

## ROUND SEVEN

I walk up to Black Mamba also known as me, also known as Willem Floures, a fighter past his prime but still doing whatever it takes to seize the spotlight; I walk up to myself and I say, "Open up, let your guard down."

## ARE YOU LISTENING?

Yes. I am.
So, why don't you "let your guard down?"
What's the worst that could happen?

## ARE YOU LISTENING?

Let your guard down!
No one is going to do any favors. I have to be the one to get the job done. I start with the jab, purposefully hitting to the gloves, warming up to the combination left, left, right, right, mix-up of straights and hooks.

The more punches I throw, the more worked up I get.
I see Mamba's body wince with every blow.
The audience continues to cheer; every moment is as exciting as the one before it. Hearing their laughter only makes me angrier.

I begin to treat Black Mamba like a punching bag.
The entire round he buckles with every single punch. I should

be feeling what he's feeling but, thanks to the adrenaline surging through my body, I won't feel it until much later.

I return to my corner thirty seconds before the end of the round, just in time to see what I've done to Mamba.

He bleeds down the right side of his face and each breath he takes is pained, the evident wheeze of a winded fighter can be heard from my corner.

Spencer and crew begin tending to my body.

Wipe the blood away.

Tend to the cut on my right side.

I breathe out, my breath loud enough to drown out Spencer's barks.

## ARE YOU LISTENING?

This is the round where the illusion shatters.

This is the round where it ends.

This is the round where the confusion becomes cataclysm.

This is the round where something in my head ruptures, and the rendered image I am left with in the aftermath of this fight is less than the sum of both victory and media regard.

They see me as that fighter; I see myself as that husk of a being, idle and dead on his feet, standing in the middle of the ring.

This is where I hurt myself, and the injury lasts a lifetime.

## ROUND EIGHT

I am listening.

I am listening to their laughter, their applause. Though I know it's genuine, I also know that it's not for me. It might be directed towards me, but it isn't for me; rather, it's for the 'Willem Floures's they have come to expect via all the publicity, every single video clip, interview, and sound bite given to the media for sculpting. They see the identity as brand rather than identity as person. I could be competitively dancing. I could be a pornstar. I could be a prostitute. I could be a slave under sinister purposes. The root isn't important:

It's what they think of you and the media's portrayal provides the impression.

I am a fighter.

I am lost on my feet as I gain their undivided favor.

And it's only because, well you know why, but I'll say it again.

I'll say it again, just to prove to myself that I'm listening.

I am interesting to them because they haven't figured me out. The enigma, the walking contradiction that is 'Sugar' Willem Floures, is one that has yet to be analyzed. From suspected murderer to suspected philanthropist, I am every much a threat to humanity as I am an asset.

Really though, I'm just a fighter, about to knock myself out.

So then let me show you how to fight before I go lights out.

## ARE YOU LISTENING?

I am asking you. Hmm?

I hope so. This is valuable advice.

Anyone can fight but only a few can win.

## JAB

You have the jab. Ease in with this punch.

This is a punch that should, like a gun, be the full extension of your arm. You reach out and test the waters. You create opportunities. You create volume; you create room between you and your opponent.

The jab is your ruler, your ability to measure and feel out the nature of the fight.

## STRAIGHT

A powerful straight punch, often dealt with your rear hand. This is why the "one-two" is a classic building block for fight momentum.

One—a jab with your lead hand.

Two—a straight with your rear hand.

I mix up my combinations with a number of "one-two"

combinations. The straight, or sometimes called a "cross," is one of the most effective punches if hit flush and with full extension (of power).

## HOOK

My favorite.

A mixture of left and right hooks to the body and face can, and will, confuse your opponent.

I can throw a left hook to the body like this...see?

And sure Mamba braces and ultimately blocks it but if I follow it up with a right hook to the body and then a right hook to the side of his head, the mix-up can affect his ability to defend.

Did you see how he kind of took the right hook to the face?

Hooks are great for rapid succession.

Like the name implies, it is a punch that involves the outward extension of your arm in a sweeping motion.

This isn't to be confused with a haymaker (I'll end with that too. Going to send him to the canvas with one).

Hooks are quick and massive. They bridge the gap between straights and uppercuts. The perfect combination, in my opinion, begins with a jab, dispenses with hooks and follows it up with an uppercut.

You throw a few straights in there for good measure.

The hook is what often wears down the ribs and body of your opponent.

Every time I punch Mamba...like so...his abdominal muscles absorb the punch. At first it is fine; that's why fighters condition their bodies, often taking round after round of punches to the stomach as conditioning.

Note to self, I need to train more.

There's often no time, what with all the booked events.

It's always something I feel guilty about. Take one look at my old and beaten body and you see a lifetime of fighting. There's still tone, still muscle, but it's hidden under layers of flab.

But anyway, that's why I can't afford to take too many punches to the body. It's why Mamba, though he looks in perfect shape, will feel it as much as I would feel it getting punched to the body repeatedly.

Eventually the abdominal muscles get sore and when they do the ribcage is no longer protected from each punch.

Each punch straight to the bone.

## UPPERCUT

Crowd pleaser. The uppercut. It's also incredibly difficult to use effectively. Most fighters can see it coming from a mile away. This kind of punch is popularized by all of the different leagues and all of the different fighters that have successfully landed the uppercut to end the fight.

It often does.

Reason being that the uppercut, if connected well, hits right under the chin. Get hit right under the chin and it's lights out.

I'll explain why.

## FOOTWORK/DEFENSE

You can't just stand there and take punches!

You can't just assume that the punches won't hurt you. Half the time it isn't about one decimating punch but rather a volume of punches over the course of the fight that causes the inevitable loss (via decision or knockout—either way it is still a loss).

Basic fighting stance—

Keep your fists up.

Keep your chin down.

You keep your chin tucked in and down because you are most vulnerable there and on either side of your head (temple shots are deadly).

The more likely a punch will cause your brain to rock back and forth inside your skull, the more likely you will get knocked out.

Get hit under the chin and the impact is like your own personal earthquake.

## HAYMAKER

And for the final punch, one that is the most common because it's the one that people use by default, and by people I mean everyone; this is the punch of a drunkard, the punch of an angry individual.

It is the punch that requires zero training.

I'd say this is the one punch that hurts the most.

Too bad it often hurts the person throwing the punch too.

How to throw a haymaker...

There is no "how."

Just throw it. Like so—

And if it connects, like it does with Black Mamba, right to the side of his head, it's lights out for him.

Meaning it's lights out for me too.

If it weren't for the boxing gloves, I would have broken my hand.

Either way, the referee, nonexistent until now, appears near Black Mamba's fading body.

The count begins.

The audience has been cheering, laughing, howling, the entire time.

I return to my corner.

The same series of actions repeated:

Spencer shouting, spit, take in water, and exhale.

### ARE YOU LISTENING?

And I'll say—yes.

Totally. If only because it's the one answer I have yet to give.

Hey, can I ask you a question?

What do I look like right about now?

# THE SILENCE I DECIDE

Now that I'm here, I can't get myself to go back out there. I should. They want to see me. I'm the talk of the industry, and maybe the whole country.

Number one fighter—'Sugar' Willem Floures.

Not that it matters much.

They are all disappearing; every time I look away, they disappear.

Them—

All of the would-be better versions of me, disappearing.

All I'm left with is myself, free from self-improvement but fixed in time with nothing to look forward to without looking back.

And I don't know where they are going. I don't know where they've gone. They know everything, though. Wherever they are, I am no longer. They replace me, showing the world that I'm a fraud. I get the last laugh though, because if they tell anyone, they only end up hurting themselves.

Their identity is my identity.

Spoil mine, spoil yours.

So they better lean towards silence if they don't want to hear the world's laughter.

### HEY, ARE YOU THERE?

He knew.

*We* knew.

What was his alias?

No, not Executioner. The other guy.

### BLACK MAMBA

## THAT'S THE ONE
## MAMBA? YOU THERE?

I don't hear anything. The house settles, exhales a low rumble, and the basement's temperature lowers, cold enough to be a chiller.

I look away just to see if another will escape.

Thankfully a few seem to have fallen asleep. I could definitely use some sleep but if I did they'd all disappear. Funny to think I haven't yet explored why they disappear at all. Is it because I am fulfilled, exactly who I want to be?

Is it because I'm satisfied with the end result of the fight?

Is it because I now understand who I am, or is it because, as number one in the league, there is irrefutable proof that I am Willem Floures? I am number one, which means the world considers me the peak of the identity. No one else is quintessentially 'Willem Floures's as I am, and that has nothing to do with the fact that maybe I started the league. Maybe I am the first to be Willem Floures.

Maybe I'm not. I don't feel like I need to know the difference.

Fact: What's my name?

There you go.

## HEY, ARE YOU THERE?

I tend to the TV. Someone has to watch the TV; otherwise, it'll cease to exist. The same goes with the people that populate each show. If there aren't enough viewers, their shows will be cancelled; their careers will suffer. They won't receive as many offers, auditions. Their futures will be a future with less work, fewer opportunities. Their lives will reflect their identities: narrow, negligible. It's why you really want to put yourself out there. You want to do whatever it takes to make that name, your identity, be a brand that is immediately recognizable.

Look at me:

Spewing media-speak.

It sounds like I'm delivering the intro to a seminar on brand awareness.

I'm way too drowsy, too high on the painkillers they gave me, to be taken seriously. At this moment, my body looks like a battlefield post-airstrike.

But I feel absolutely nothing.

Everything I hear echoes out like it's being repeated by two separate voices. Everything I watch is in slow motion. This movie on TV is supposed to be nonstop action but I really think it would have been more effective if the action star ran faster, the death scenes more plentiful, and the explosions a little less exaggerated. But hey—

It's just my opinion.

Maybe not even that...

It could be the painkillers.

### HEY, ARE YOU THERE?

What?

### HUH?

Are you there?

### AM I WHERE?

What?

### WHO'S TALKING?

I was going to ask you the same question.

### WHAT?

What?

### WHAT IS GOING ON?

What?

## STOP TALKING

Okay.

## GOOD

Where do we go from here? I tune into the silence of the basement. Look over my shoulder and notice that one more has disappeared. That leaves seventeen left. I admit that I don't feel much of anything at the moment. The impossibility of their kidnapping right on down to the impossibility of the numbness I feel somehow having something to do with their disappearance:

It registers at face value.

The inherent value being...not very much. Apparently.

Carrying the numbness, the most I can manage is keeping my focus on the TV and so that's what I do. Through the haze of painkillers, the movie either ends or my attention span splinters to nothing.

Whatever happens I end up flipping channels every thirty seconds.

Meanwhile I bask in the silence I have decided to be the most perfect victory. I pass by one of the sports channels where, big surprise, they are talking about the fight like it was a barnburner.

Did it really look like a barnburner?

Hmm?

Special mention of both of our aliases.

## HEY, ARE YOU THERE?

No answer of course because whoever's left is right here in the basement with me. The rest of the league is out to get me. That is, to say, the majority vote being against the idea that I have made some great accomplishment.

I turn to them, "Hey...have I accomplished anything?"

No answer because I haven't.

No answer because their mouths are taped.

No answer because I decide the nature of the silence and I've decided that it should be all encompassing.

If I am unable to understand, I don't want to be able to feel.

If I am unable to feel, I don't want to see anything that'll remind me of what I've mentioned above.

If I am unable to see, I certainly don't want to hear anything. I just want to watch TV.

Watch other identities take the spotlight.

Skip to the next sports channel.

They analyze the version of the fight that didn't happen. If they had been watching, and I mean really watching, they would have blocked it from memory much like I did.

The only evidence of victory (and loss) is my beaten, broken body.

Fact: It's the same as any fight.

Their favor always fades long before I can recuperate.

## I DON'T KNOW

That being said, *I don't really know* how I got here.

I must have been treated in order to get like this.

Picture: the IV hooked to my veins, the dosage and documentation of how much to take, the gurney, the nurse spoon-feeding me, the neutral white, the sighting of blood bleeding through the dressings.

To get here, I must have gone through a lot.

I am the spotlight and no matter what I do to try to relish in the satisfaction of having reclaimed my title spot, "number one," the designation registers as meaningless to me. It doesn't help make any better sense of what I've slaughtered. I worked so hard, did so much, to get here.

But am I any clearer of my objective?

My purpose?

Who I am?

What is this supposed to be for?

## I DON'T KNOW

Exactly. I am a lapse of everything but what the TV tells me.

There are sit-coms telling me to laugh and surely there are news channels telling me all about my accolades. They call me a fighter, a real pugilist celebrity.

Sure enough I am, to them, but for how long?

How ironic to discover that the achievement is nowhere near as satisfying as the fight to get there.

I try to remember what it felt like when I was younger, achieving so much at such a young age, and remaining undefeated for such a long time; however, where there should be reason I am left with basic facts.

I won.

And my fight record.

League stats.

I always focused on what I hadn't achieved rather than what I managed to become. Especially now, where everything is consistently muted and disengaged from the actual circumstances, I am essentially living more in my head than out in the open. I switch the channels but nothing registers as anything more than a set of images, colors, and criticism.

They favor me, but what does that even mean?

Tomorrow it'll be different.

Tomorrow might be like yesterday—

Full of uncertainty and the discussion of a follow-up fight where I am the potential underdog (he's old—he's not what he used to be) and every lie, every single time I shilled to become significant, will have gone to waste.

## I DON'T KNOW

It's true. I don't know what's happened and I don't know what'll happen. I don't want to look back at them because I know the number will have dwindled at least by two.

What will they do?

## I DON'T KNOW

What will I do besides watch TV?

Isn't that enough? After you are in a fight where you are

beaten into a bloody pulp, watching TV is the perfect answer to "what do you do?"

I switch from a soap opera to a talk show.

"On how they got a second chance."

Tell me about the world, TV.

Tell me why I'm watching you.

The host brings a bunch of celebrities past their prime onto the stage. Together they televise the basic message that has existed as an unsung law of sorts in our culture.

An identity is like a person in that it has to continually change and evolve to stay alive. One step further—

A person is an identity.

When hasn't this been the case?

Much like a roundtable discussion, they tip-toe around the basics and they barely get their point across to the audience before they have to cut to a commercial break. Tantamount to a knockout, a commercial break is suicide to the momentum of a debate.

When they return, they talk more about themselves. They use the opportunity to be on camera as a means of promoting their next projects.

As I watch, I see the celebrities not as different identities but as different versions of myself, talking feverishly about their relevancy.

Prove to the world that you matter.

I switch channels.

Watch the world go by with a single step up from twelve to thirteen on the dial.

I cough and I can feel the house cough with me, trembling at the foundation. I close my eyes and feel the resonating pull into the grey that the medication makes me feel.

I reopen my eyes and I feel like I've lost something else.

What was it like to win the title?

## I DON'T KNOW

Back to the TV, the window into the outside world, and it's already reached middle age. If I had my phone, I would have favored that window over this one. I can barely move; my arms feel heavy. My legs…I'm not even going to try to walk at this point. Someone sat me here in front of the TV.

This is where I will continue to sit.

What happened to…

# I DON'T KNOW

I forgot what I was about to ask.

What am I trying to say?

# I DON'T KNOW

This is the kind of confusion that I am not used to. It's not a waking confusion; it is the kind of confusion that renders my memory useless. At least before, I wouldn't know until a few triggers recovered the item from the so-called archive of my battle-tired brain.

However, so numbed out by the medication, I am barely alive.

I am barely alive at a time when I could be considered someone that is the most alive. At this very moment, my worth is skyrocketing and I can do nothing to care.

Why?

# I DON'T KNOW

That is good enough of a reason.

I will not be able to enjoy my achievement.

Never have, never will.

And I could worry about what they will do to reclaim some of the spotlight. I might wonder about Executioner and Lights Out and Buster and Ice and…and…and…and…and… But not Black Mamba; he is as bad off as I am, trading comments, sharing the same internal monologue that lately sounds more like a machine than a human voice.

Change the channel.

Change the channel.

Change the channel.

Change the channel.

## QUIET!

I hear it droning on and on and it gets to a point where I am on the verge of being irritated before a distraction, as if on cue, pulls me out of the definite haze.

I hear footsteps upstairs.

Right on cue.

I look over at them.

Three more gone. That leaves fourteen.

I struggle to my feet. It's a lot like watching a zombified version of your body from over one of your shoulders. It's like I'm holding the game controller and I am directing my next move with every press of the button.

I shuffle my way to their side of the basement.

I tear the tape off X's mouth.

I lean in close and it takes me a long time to finally say what I want to say, "Did...did...you *hear*...something?"

X's tired eyes, his sunken skin, his horrible deathly breath as he says:

"You..."

I want to ask him what he means but that'll take too much energy.

I'm lucky enough to have asked him anything.

And besides, X's eyes roll back in his skull, collapsing against the harness, hanging there, circling the drain of death.

The fourteen that remain, they are young but ill.

They are versions of me that remain only because I've moved on. I have outlived their goals, their lives made, met, and finally matriculated to the point of losing momentum. My way of saying they would have followed in my footsteps, not wanting to change anything.

The ones that escape me are the ones that think they can do better.

Haven't I done well enough for myself?

## I DON'T KNOW

Each stair is excruciating when your knees buckle and your body does not want to cooperate.

The sounds coming from upstairs, just above me, are all that keeps me going. The footsteps sound like mine. Somewhere in this house, I will recover a few basic facts about myself. Namely, I will figure out why *they* escape and why I feel like I've lost a part of myself at the same time that I should feel like I am complete, a champion, a celebrity.

I should find out how it all ends because everything comes to an end if it's anything of value. That's why I cling to my brand.

Willem Floures lives on forever.

But what about me?

It's selfish, I know.

That's something else I'll recover, the fact that I am self-absorbed.

## I DON'T KNOW

"I don't know" is a placeholder hanging with the drug-induced numbness of the past week. I haven't so much as left the basement since leaving the hospital. I've failed to really grasp the events of the week before.

I reach the door to the basement and after taking a couple heavy breaths, I step into the kitchen. The comfort of the house is never more apparent than in the kitchen and adjoining dining and family rooms.

Recover: the memories of spending long nights watching movies, analyzing fight footage, and smoking cigars in the family room while Sarah Mullen ran around playing various imaginative games, often mixing drinks for Spencer and I.

Recover: the memories of Spencer Mullen, my only friend, longtime agent and trainer.

It's all starting to snap into place.

Recover: the memories of the fight between Executioner and I.

Recover: the memories of public spectacle, "I KILLED A MAN."

Recover: the memories of Spencer paying off the authorities, keeping them quiet on the fact that it was a lie. No man murdered. No man harmed.

Recover: the memory of a recent argument with a certain someone.

The medicated numbness pulls back as I am reminded of what's missing.

Recover: the memory of Spencer being absent from recent events, Spencer and the kidnappings; the kidnappings and how they are escaping and what that might mean for Spencer and our professional relationship and the friendship as a whole.

Recover: enough to send me into a sprint around the house, listening for those footsteps.

I run to one end of the hall and wait.

Listen.

I hear footsteps trailing behind me, stopping, mimicking my own.

Don't move. Wait.

The footsteps begin up the steps to the second floor. Each step creaks with deliberate purpose. Direct me to where I need to be.

I run up the steps, feeling nauseous due to the increase in heart-rate after having been medicated and stationary for so long.

I really shouldn't be running around like this, not while on this sort of medication, but who's going to stop me? Myself?

Yeah right.

No trust there.

The second floor hallway is lightless and dark.

The stairs continue to creak long after I've climbed them.

Annoyed, I shout:

## QUIET!

And the house is still.

Tune into the atmosphere. I merge into the cadence of the house.

I open the one door that leads to the one room that matters most.

Sarah sits in a rocking chair, talking to herself, "Yeah it's going to be a great day! I like swing sets!"

She sees me and I freeze, as if not wanting to be found out.

She continues talking, "He's finally here.

"Yeah he looks better than he was.

"Yeah he doesn't know.

"Yeah he's not going to take the news very well."

I make a face, "What are you doing? Stop talking to yourself!"

Sarah tilts her head to one side, "Look who's talking."

"Yeah he hasn't noticed."

"What? *What?*"

Sarah addresses the area to her left, "Should I tell him?"

I shake my head, "Is it James again? More of your imaginary friends?"

Sarah replies with an even tone, "Dad says you need to start listening if you want to keep the story going."

You can say I'm a little startled, "What do you mean?"

I look around the room, "Who are you talking to?"

Taking a few steps forward, "Who are you talking to Sarah?"

Sarah says, "Dad wants to know if you remember anything?"

"Spencer?"

Sarah nods, "He's right here."

"Where?"

"Dad says you can't see him."

"But you can?"

Sarah grins, "You wrote him out of your life. He doesn't exist anymore."

"I don't..." I trail off, shaking my head.

Recall what I said about confusion. It's all coming back to me now.

"Dad says he's teaching James how to box like a well-rounded fighter."

"What?"

She nods, "Yeah, Dad says James can be even better than you. Dad says he's more dedicated."

What I feel isn't quite anger but it's not far off.

"Dad says he's even got a good alias for James."

"Oh yeah, and what is it?"

"Dad says it's 'Dynamite.'"

Her words send shivers down my spine.

I sit down on the edge of her bed.

I listen to Sarah talk to her father, getting only one side of the conversation. Amid the space of a haunting, Spencer has sought revenge for being unwritten from my career.

And yes, I did that.

I ignored him.

I didn't appreciate him.

What is James but another imposter?

# THE SILENCE I DESIGN

It's not what I choose to remember but rather that I remembered anything at all. When everything eventually falls silent, the fact that I can retain the texture of a surface and the pitch of a tone, the smell of a scent and the resonance of an emotion, is more than enough. I should be content that I am able to retain any fragment of my past. I mean, right?

That's why we have photo albums, flash drives, and home videos.

What else am I missing?

The silence I design comes from the memories I derive.

## SILENCE

In each moment of silence, I pull from a memory I never knew I had.

They haunt me like the hauntings continue to linger around the house. I no longer question whether the hauntings or the memories are real or fake. The fact that they remain in my mind is enough and I hope it is enough for you.

But then why Spencer, why now?

Why James, who does he think he is?

## SILENCE

"He seems to think he'll be a better version of you," Sarah says. She sneaks up behind me, grabs my hand, looks at my reflection in her vanity mirror. I look down at her and ask, "So you hear them then? It wasn't your imagination?"

She grins, "Do you want to play a game?"

When I turn to look back at myself in the mirror, I discover that my reflection is already staring back at me.

"Umm…"

Sarah looks, "Oh, you can see him! Yay!"

"What?"

"James, say hi!"

My reflection steps to the side, waves and says, "Hello, my name's Willem."

I hear him, his voice tinny and muffled but otherwise it's a lot like listening to your voice after having been recorded on a cheap microphone.

Sarah giggles, "I still like to call him James."

"I was James, once," he nods, winking at Sarah.

"That's me? That doesn't look like me!"

## SILENCE

"Dad says that it does."

"Where is he?"

"Dad says he's standing right next to you."

I rub my eyes but nothing changes the fact that I can't see him. So what happens next? What turns James into me?

"Don't you remember?"

What do I say to that?

What does she even mean?

A rumble comes from deeper in the house. The basement.

Sarah gasps, "He let another one go."

"Spencer?"

She nods, "Dad is mad at you."

"Tell him I'm mad at him!"

Sarah frowns, "I don't think you and Dad should fight so much."

## DO I HAVE A CHOICE?

Does anyone have a choice?

I feel like the values around me change more often than I can create meaning. What am I?

List them here:

————————————
————————————
————————————

Because lately, due to the last fight and what I've done to create a fence around the spotlight, everyone has been wanting to create their own definition of who I am. Who is Willem Floures?

It's not an easy question to answer.

Not something easily defined.

Then again, can any identity be clearly defined?

Sarah says, "Dad thinks you are too self-absorbed."

"Really?"

Nodding, "And Dad says that you could have been a better fighter if you did more for yourself instead of…" she stops, as if waiting for the rest of it to be whispered into her ear, "having him speak for you."

"Tell him that's absolute bullshit. He wanted as much of the spotlight as he could manage!"

Sarah replies, "Dad says he can hear you fine. Dad also says that you should have started writing your story if you wanted to be the biggest part of it."

I shrug, "What does that even mean?"

James chimes in, "Own every decision you make. Nothing just 'happens' without there being a sequence of actions and reactions."

"I wasn't talking to you."

"If you aren't talking to me then you're clearly in denial. You need to start listening to what you're saying."

Sarah tells me, "Dad says that you need to stop hiding from what's happened."

"What? What does he mean by that? I think I've seen too much as it is. I feel like I might forget how to breathe, that's how confused and blurred everything has become!"

Sarah lets go of my hand.

Everything goes silent.

## SILENCE

And within the silence, something climbs out of a far-off

cavern of my mind. My eyes cross, vision blurring, until I blink in rapid succession.

Eyes uncrossed, I see in the mirror an entire memory on replay where I am seemingly the only one that hasn't seen it before.

## SILENCE

The memory plays out like a silent film.

The faces I make are extremely exaggerated. I am not fighting myself. I am fighting everyone else. The ring is more of a stage dressed up to look like a ring. There must be a number of cameras because the angle switches often enough to account for at least five distinct, separate sources.

I see a number of shots, all of them haymakers from one young man.

Not me.

I am not young.

The camera cuts to where Spencer would be standing, but he is not there. The silent film cuts to the word MISSING and back to the memory.

Memory has a runtime of a couple of minutes.

Memory is a scene in a film everyone watched but me.

The young man hits me with a haymaker that must have hurt him more than it hurt me, but like a nice guy (really?) I seem to fake a KO.

I fall to the floor and a woman dressed as a referee, who appears to be the host of this memory, this talk show of some sort, begins the ten count, stops at five, lifts me up, sees that I'm totally "KOed" and waves her arms.

No contest.

The young man in pain is treated a prize.

Cut to the words:

## WE HAVE A WINNER!

Next frame:

## YOU KO'ED THE TOP CONTENDER!

Next frame:

## WHAT IS HENRY'S LAST WISH?

Cut back to the memory.

Cut back to film: The cameras zoom in close on the young man. He appears malnourished, barely anything but skin and bones. He doesn't have any hair. The host hugs him; Henry grips his hand, in pain, but is too excited by the win, the ultimate prize (anything he wants).

Cuts away before I can get a look at what he wanted.

## SILENCE

In that moment of silence the mirror fades to black and the house mutes itself as I reflect on what I just saw.

It rushes at me, the details.

"Make a Wish Foundation: Day of Fisticuffs: Sponsored by _____: Live on The Day Show. All proceeds go to terminal cancer research."

## SILENCE

The mirror holds more.

I try to look away but can't: I want to remember.

I want to see.

This one has sound.

No color. I seem to remember things in a debilitated, limited manner.

There is only sound and the still image of my face.

That's me?

I look tired, dark bags under the eyes, my eyes barely open. I have my hand raised, as if swatting away some sort of unpleasantness.

There is static.

## SILENCE

And then the audio begins and the moment it begins I want it to stop.

How do I forget?

Hear: "...yeah. Yeah. No, that's not it at all. Like, I know that I've had a great career but fuck them if they think I'm nearing the end. I'm like fine wine, with age comes an onslaught, you know?"

Static over everyone else's voice but mine.

"Yeah! Exactly."

Static.

"This? It's just a little confidence. Sipping confidence. Sipping confidence like it's nothing really. No. I don't remember anything about that."

Static.

"So what? Maybe I dabbled in the charities. It looks good when you're in with the charities. Huh? I don't know what I'm talking about half the time. Sipping confidence and slinging punches. That's what it's all about."

Static.

"You're talking to me. Nothing but 'Sugar.' Willem's the name and Floures is the game."

I cringe; grind my teeth the more I listen.

## SILENCE

Thankfully it ends but not before the fade to black, the surge of residual remembrance. It was some kind of provocative morning radio show.

The word "uncensored" comes to mind.

I sound like an asshole and maybe that's what I was aiming for at the time. I remember bits and pieces about how the media was baffled by the performance, summing it up as "tell-all" and "inebriated and grilled by XXXX" the radio DJ who I can't seem to remember by name.

I can see him though, what he looks like.

He passes through the mirror; I see him walking by

Yeah, that's him.

I mean, my appearance is unbearable and really humiliating but maybe that was the point?

I don't know…

I don't feel good about it.

It makes me look like…

## SILENCE

The memories are mine.

They begin to speak to me in a voice that's familiar but I can't yet place where I've heard it before.

The colors bleed into each other as I watch two faces form—mine and…another familiar face.

Cut to a frame, made entirely for reference:

## HE IS A CELEBRITY, OKAY?

Okay.

Bleed more until I see the surrounding, the context, the nature of this promotional media event.

## CELEBRITY FIGHT NIGHT

I am fighting someone that's never fought before. Not in this context. The memory trickles out like yet another fragment of film.

Perspective is a set of eyes is a single camera is a handy-cam, somewhat grainy quality. At one point the camera is flipped around so that I can see into myself. At that moment I see a flicker of myself, 'James,' Sarah, and someone else. A reflection of selves haunting anomalous spaces.

That someone else is Spencer. But I don't know that until after everything falls back to silence.

The celebrity and I trade punches but it's clear that I'm not having it.

I focus on the jab, taking it easy for a few rounds, until the celebrity hits me with a hook that pushes through my some-what shoddy defense and stuns me. Off center, the celebrity actually scores a knockdown.

The audience erupts.

The laughter sends familiar shivers down my spine.

## AUDIENCE
## LAUGHING

I feel as cold as I must have felt at the time. Shivering, I don't realize how angry I am. I saunter over to the celebrity and hit him right in the head.

Decent punch to the face while the celebrity's fists were down. The memory bleeds into each argument, the verbal quarrel that transpires afterwards. Bleed into one of the later rounds, after the argument ends but isn't settled, and the fight isn't just a promotional fight anymore; the celebrity is out for blood. Blood drips from a cut right below the celebrity's right eyebrow and that is what the camera focuses on.

Something is wrong here:

If the camera isn't how I saw it, who is holding the camera?

Who stood to my right in the ring, circling around us like a VIP cameraman while I targeted the cut, sending punch after punch right for the same spot, hoping to open the wound enough to leave a scar (and maybe end the celebrity's career as an actor)?

## SILENCE

The memory continues to bleed with or without any sense.

The celebrity doesn't know how to control emotion during a fight and I take advantage of that. You can't let anger fuel the fight; it can be an influence, sure, but if you are throwing volume punches with no other strategy, your opponent will stop your would-be freight-train long before the fight can go the distance.

The cut is looking bad; bad enough that celebrity blood bleeds into the memory and ruins the end of the fight.

I might have won the fight but it bleeds into the aftermath. Ambulance ride for both celebrity and I.

Bleed.

Somewhere later, we sit facing a set of cameras. Bright lights wash out the blood, wash out any words that we might have said.

It looks bad.

I look better than the celebrity, but it is clear that the publicity stunt went wrong. Maybe it went right. I don't seem to recall.

The memory continues to bleed out the final clause:

And I hear it as a single sentence, a question, directed at me, from a media representative as baffled as anyone else, "What is wrong with you?"

The memory bleeds until black.

And then there is...

### SILENCE

I want to say something but this is not the time or place to say much of anything. I've already spoken for myself. For better and for worse, I outstepped any logic, any reasonable understanding based on the identity as it used to be.

Blink.

A frame appears, sans memory:

### ARTICLE TITLE: THE RISE AND FALL OF WILLEM FLOURES

### ARTICLE TITLE: THE TRUTH ABOUT 'SUGAR' WILLEM FLOURES: INTERVIEW WITH A CIPHER

### ARTICLE TITLE: THE GOLDEN AGE OF FISTICUFFS: IS IT OVER?

### ARTICLE TITLE: THE SECRETS AND LIES EXPOSED: A GROUP INTERVIEW WITH THE FIGHTERS OF WILLEM FLOURES

A frame breaks into shards before the next memory wipes the mirror clean. The memory has both color and sound.

The memory takes place in a large arena, full of pyrotechnics, fans holding makeshift signs, many of them praising an identity that isn't mine, and I have full control of the ring.

I hold a microphone and, so unlike me (what does that even mean anymore?), I provoke the audience.

The words "heel" and "sports entertainment" and "celebrity walk-on" flicker in between frames.

The memory aligns to what I imagine are the official broadcast cameras. I see myself for what I really look like. Outside of any self-created visage, that is me…and I look a lot like 'James.'

It looks like 'James' is filling in for me.

"I'm here to save all you idiot wrestling fans from wasting more brain cells watching a *fake* fight!"

## AUDIENCE
## LAUGHTER

Provokes me.

Their laughter is what I want to change.

I don't want to hear it. As the memory begins to reveal itself, I struggle to ignore, to look away, anything, just:

No more of it.

Please.

But it seems the memory is a portrayal of the same self-conscious person that I am. The laughter switches to cheers, chaotic chanting, because it seems that I appeared at the venue for one reason and one reason only:

I am there to beat up 'Sugar' Willem Floures.

Not just any part of myself—

I am there to beat up the most vulnerable part of me.

"Is that what you want?!"

The memory skips, already winded, out of breath from twelve rounds of a fight that should have never transpired.

## IS THAT WHAT YOU WANT?!

Then that's what I give them.

Punch to the stomach.

Punch to the face.

That gets a big enough reaction.

Punch to the face, to the stomach.
Punch to the mouth.
Punch to the stomach, to the stomach, to the stomach.
Punch to the eye.
Eye closes shut.
Punch to the eye.
Punch to the mouth, to the face, to the stomach.
Punch to the forehead.
The memory skips, fading to black.

## SILENCE

I breathe heavily.
The black fades back to our reflection.
And that's what makes it all click into place.
The voice narrating every single memory…
It's Spencer's.
The memories comprise his own sort of mourning for the Willem he once knew. Every single memory is familiar not only because they are mine but also because they were the subject of Spencer's lectures long after I stopped listening. I wonder:

If I had continued to listen and take notes, would Spencer have continued to discuss boxing?

Would his lectures have continued to analyze my fight performance rather than my performance as myself, as the identity I confuse and abuse?

Have I done something grave?

Willem Floures as enigma, does it fail to be as prominent as Willem Floures the boxer?

## SILENCE

Of course I have no one to consult but myself. They all seem to know what's right even if we know that it's wrong.

I look at Sarah.

I look at 'James.'

I look at myself and it's a lot like looking at the reflection of a stranger.

A knot of dread in my gut worsens when Spencer walks into frame.

Right there, in the mirror, Sarah's claims are correct.

I wrote him out of my "story."

I look at my reflection.

## THAT'S ME?
## THAT DOESN'T LOOK LIKE ME

Spencer replies, voice an echo in my mind, "How would you know?"

# THE SILENCE I DROVE

There is rhythm to any mania. Maybe it's the mania that sets the rhythm and makes it impossible for me to keep up.

Some identities don't have much else but the voice, no career source, no means of buoying their celebrity stake of the spotlight besides their ability to surprise. And maybe that's why I drove myself to silence during the early, younger, golden years of my boxing career.

I used to think silence would be enticing; only now, do I realize that silence is worthless unless it precedes or follows a storm.

## SILENCE

It's all I'm left with. Bask in silence of a basement where only X and I remain. The rest have escaped. They've taken any clear sense of what I can be. Spencer let them out as effortlessly as he led them here, tethered and tied. I pick at the scab of a memory where I confronted Spencer about his actions. I don't remember what was said but I recall it had something to do with jealousy.

Perhaps it was guilt. Whatever it was, it is no more.

Left behind the silence and the solace I ignore.

I have nowhere else to go.

With the TV on full-blast, I keep myself entertained.

I drive the silence away.

The TV pays me back for having paid so much attention to it.

The house doesn't make a move, too afraid it'll get my attention; I need to be alone. I need to think about this. I need to avoid it for the time being.

Wait until this show is over.

Not now. Maybe after the next one.

It's only thirty minutes.
There's plenty of time.
Right X?

## BREAKING NEWS

The show I'm watching, the show that's watching me, is interrupted by a loud crescendo of over-produced brass instrumentation.

I try turning the volume down but there's no remote.

"Hey X, you have the remote over there by any chance?"

Executioner sits in the chair next to me, slouching, eyes open and cloudy; he's quiet even though I set him free myself.

Really, he was the one that should have taken my place.

I can't believe I'm saying this but…he would have carried the Willem Floures name well.

It's because I can't find the remote that I am stuck watching the one channel at the current volume.

The news anchor with a well-rehearsed grin begins, "We interrupt our regularly scheduled program with an update from an already-in-progress press conference between league officials on what will be the follow-up to last month's fight. We bring you there, live—"

## RECOGNIZABLE FACES
## SPENCER
## 'JAMES'
## ME
## 'SPENCER'

I turn and look at where they had all been tied down. No one left.

I count up from two, reassessing how many there had been versus how many were never caught. I give up somewhere around twenty.

I ask X, "What do you make of this? If I am here, who is that?"

X blinks.

The press conference is most definitely breaking news.

Then 'Spencer' speaks for 'me' making boastful claims about how the new contender, 'Dynamite,' but who I'll always call 'James,' is yet another wannabe, just someone who hopes to ride the coat tails of a 'G.O.A.T.'

G.O.A.T.
THE ACRONYM STANDS FOR:
GREATEST
OF
ALL
TIME

Whatever it is that's supposed to be me doesn't speak.

Just like I had been prior to my fight for the spotlight. I'm not sure which version was better. At the very least, I was entertaining and memorable. The loss of reality and self had to be for something, right?

'James' shadowboxes while Spencer expertly dodges and weaves 'Spencer's' claims.

The 'Spencer' of the past cannot contend with the Spencer of today.

'James' what do you have to say?

I say: You can't replace me.

I say: You can try but you'll fail.

What I really say is nothing.

I am a voyeur, watching from behind a dusty plasma TV screen.

"Hey X, if that's supposed to be me, then who the hell am I? Who the hell are you?"

X blinks.

"I'm starting to sense that you're trying to use some kind of Morse code using blinks. I don't know if I'll follow."

BLINK ONCE FOR "YES"

BLINK TWICE FOR "NO"

## BLINK THREE TIMES FOR "IDIOT"

"That's our code, okay?"

The conference continues with banter from Spencer and 'Spencer.' Spencer toys with 'Spencer,' successfully summarizing the fight plan because it's a strategy we used back during my twenty-first fight. Or was it my twenty-second?

"X?"

He blinks.

I don't catch how many times.

'Spencer' answers questions addressed for Spencer.

Both 'me' and 'James' stand off to the side, arms crossed, the effect a fighter is looking to achieve at one of these press conferences is intimidation.

Intimidate your opponent.

Intimidate yourself.

The conference ends with an official press release:

SUGAR VS. DYNAMITE
UNDERCARD:
SCORPION VS. DEADSIE
SWAGGER VS. THRILL KILL
BAD INTENTIONS VS. STINGER

Like any other fight card, it is a great night of boxing where, essentially, people get to watch me beat the shit out of myself for four hours.

"That's entertainment!"

I look over at X, waiting for a reaction.

Number of blinks: One.

I clap my hands, "Righto!"

You see, if I don't act enthusiastic I'll end up as desperately confused as I was when I first started. It will feel like the last couple fights were for nothing.

Absolutely nothing.

I can't accept such a conclusion. I have to believe that I fought for valid reasons. Even if I don't know where I stand, and I'm not quite sure if anyone can really see me, I can see myself.

I pinch the skin of my forearm.

I dig my nail into the skin, drawing blood.

I feel it. I can feel something.

No more mirrors. No more hauntings.

Just this.

I need to maintain a balance if I'm going to begin evaluating what is and what isn't—and with all of them gone and/or against me, the fight is mine to win. Even though I'm the champion, I feel like the underdog.

## DYNAMITE POISED FOR TITLE WIN

The media sweeps other coverage underneath the steady onslaught of 'James's' younger look. He's not the tattooed, scarred up, busted up and slack body that I command.

Between commercials, I look at the tattoos for some sense of direction.

## NOISE

I bask in the noise of a number of different sources.

X hasn't moved but he's still here. Despite our past, I feel like he's the only friend I have left.

I used to have a close friend, a confidant, someone that kept certain aspects of me in check but he's betrayed me, left me for someone that didn't exist until a day or two ago.

"Just because you say that he's Willem Floures doesn't make it true!"

I clear my throat, "You idiot, do you think this is how it should end?"

Spencer on TV, "Interview at Ringside," one of those inside looks at upcoming fight events from the minds of experts.

It might as well be a shout-out because I know he's talking about me.

## WHY WOULDN'T HE BE?

He's talking about *me*.

Whatever that means.

"X, help me out here!"

X blinks. Three…four times?

"What are you trying to say? I'm an idiot?"

Spencer chuckles, "Now that's a knockout of a question. I don't want to go into too much detail but the short answer is yes. What you have to understand about Willem is his propensity for expansion—be that new strategies, new campaigns, new ideas, or in this case, a new era. I really believe the same could be said about any other identity. The fight takes place not only in the ring but also in the limelight. Willem is a timeless fighter and in order to maintain that sort of commodity, he transforms himself as often as possible."

I press my nose up to the TV screen, "Those are my ideas! You fucking stole my ideas!"

Flicker of a thought—

## HOW DO YOU KNOW?

I exhale, suddenly overwhelmed by nausea, leaning back in my seat.

Spencer continues unabated, "The fight is full circle. Mind, body, and self."

Interviewer with the next question, "Is it true what they say about how a second person comes out in the ring? I don't want to resort to terms like 'inner demon' and 'animal' because…well maybe you can help clarify."

Nodding, Spencer replies, "Sure, sure and, yeah, that's a tricky one. It is difficult to describe. A fighter certainly taps into some sort of reservoir of emotion and both instinct and skill use the emotive material as fuel for the will and audacity of going twelve rounds against well…every fight is ultimately a personal one. You could be fighting an entire country but the one opponent that you have to defeat in order to win is you. Time and time again, it's always the same."

## EVERY FIGHT IS A PERSONAL ONE

I look over at X.

"Hey…"

X's eyes are closed.

"Hey…you watching this?"

Silence.

Don't leave me with silence.

I talk over the TV, talking about anything to keep from listening to the rest of the interview.

I lean back in my seat, closing my eyes.

"Hey X, remember the week before the fight. Not the second fight but the first fight. The one where you really gave me a wake-up call…

"The one where you KOed me and ended my win streak…

"The one where I didn't make it past round eight…

"The one where the media overused your alias in the merchandise, all that stuff involving a hooded executioner punching me so hard my face caves in…the fight where I felt like you were telling me what I was going to do next…the fight where I couldn't think for myself…I heard the world, and by that I mean I could hear the audience…separate voices pieced apart so that I could hear their criticism…I could hear them laughing as you sent me to the canvas for the ten count…

"Hey X…

"Do you think I wanted to lose?

"That kind of goes against everything I've done to stay relevant…

"But do you think, maybe, I am just in denial…

"Maybe I should have quit before I fought you…

"Maybe what I thought you were telling me was really what I wanted to hear…. Maybe…but, well, it's just…

"You know?"

## OPEN ENDED QUESTION

Before I can fight to stay awake, I have fallen asleep.

Dreamless and vacant, it feels like it lasts a single, solitary moment. It feels a lot like I am trying to escape myself.

But I'm not lucky enough.

I wake up to the sound of applause.

On TV, 'James' works on his footwork, shuffling left, shuffling right, to the satisfaction of a dozen media cameras poised to capture the footage for the evening news and RSS feeds populating a billion people's lives.

Cling to those feeds.

It might be the only reason you are alive.

The cameras catch sight of 'James' as he readies himself for the media sparring event, an event Spencer never allowed before.

But with 'James…'

'James' can do everything and more!

The camera close to his face as he seemingly laces up his boots, the news correspondent flatters him with voice-over introductions:

"We are here with 'Dynamite' Willem Floures, the undefeated, charismatic boxer-puncher extraordinaire, about to go five rounds with one of the best and we're capturing it all live on FightTV!"

'James' poses for the cameras. Fists up, the stare of a champion.

## FIGHT TV TOUTS:
## FIGHT PREDICTIONS

Nope—no thanks. Time to tune out. Switch the channels.

I look for the remote.

Not under the cushion. Not kicked to the side.

"Hey X, help me find the remote…"

Suddenly I hear the bell.

Years of fights have trained me to snap into action.

I jump to my feet, startled.

Fact:

## I AM STILL THE CHAMPION

Right?

The sparring session begins.

'James' has full command over the entire ring.

He leads with the jab in such a plain and straightforward

manner, I am momentarily relieved. He's predictable, an amateur.

He knows less about me than I do.

Good.

But then it all clicks into place.

He isn't a boxer-puncher.

He is a counterpuncher.

'James' dispenses with the jabs; occasionally he connects with a sharper punch. Not quite an overhand straight but not quite a jab.

But he is patient.

Waits for the other fighter to fall into a trap.

And then—

### STEP BACK
### LEAN
### COUNTER WITH A HOOK TO THE FACE

The way 'James' effortlessly takes a half-step back, clearing the reach of the strike, slightly leaning back, references the kind of lateral-momentum I used to have during the first half of my career before I injured my back.

Took one too many punches to the body.

The hook is brilliantly placed.

FightTV camera records the loud smack of glove hitting skull. It sounds like a firecracker.

### SOUNDS LIKE DYNAMITE

I haven't seen such a perfectly executed countering shot in quite some time. I don't know how I feel about this. 'James' continues the calm, confident pace for the next two rounds.

He wins on the would-be scorecards and he wows the media with such fine footwork and countering mixed offense-defense.

Perhaps most alarming is how original he is compared to the rest of us.

I can hear the media voices bragging:

### A NEW ERA

I can hear all kinds of discussion about 'James' as this century's first perfect specimen, an example of the evolution of a fighter.

I watch, completely captivated.

Edge of my seat, I say to X, "What do you think?"

## SILENCE

Silence is not a good sign.

"I think…I think…"

I watch as 'James' rolls his shoulder as the other fighter connects with a painful-looking power shot. The rolling of the shoulder is a defensive tactic that's quite difficult to master to the point where it is freely used.

"Look at that man…"

I am amazed.

The worry…

The jealousy…

The fact that 'James's' opponent, 'me,' has an impossible task ahead of him, all predates the inevitable conclusion I will soon make:

## I AM FIGHTING 'JAMES'

Don't try to figure out how this works.

I'm in the basement watching from a small TV, sulking about how my life has basically derailed itself and yet I am somehow out there, riding the scent of media glory, a facsimile of 'Sugar' Willem Floures.

I don't begin to question it.

Too much of my story is a blur of private identity made public.

I take it for what it is.

## ADMIT IT

I do—

"I enjoy watching 'James' fight. He's truly a remarkably

trained fighter. Spencer...did he actually listen to you?"

I reach over, tapping X on the shoulder, "Hey, hey X, what's your verdict?"

He is cool to the touch.

I look over and for the first time I notice the pale skin, the eyelids partially open revealing the whites of his eyes.

I let out a long sigh.

The remote is in his lap.

I lean over and grab it.

Press mute.

I reposition X to get a better look at him.

There is no pulse.

## SILENCE

I am draped in the silence of having discovered I'm all that's left.

I am all that's left of an era I had created.

The identity I defined...

The identity I defied to defend against all of them wanting their own say, their own alteration of who I am...

WHO I AM

WHO AM I

WHO

ARE

YOU

?

Executioner is dead. Feeling the nausea creep back up my throat, I fall back into my seat, palm clasped over my face.

Debilitated, I am left to the silence.

I have no way of fighting back.

## SILENCE

The silence I...

The silence...

The silence I…
Silence I…
I…
I…
I.

## SILENCE

The silence where I…fall face-first into the fields of memories buried, memories I had hidden six feet under, erased.

The silence I drove brings back a trunkful.

I shiver. I've said all that I haven't meant to say, done what I didn't mean to do. I can no longer talk about myself.

Only they can.

Only someone that can see.

Senses buckle and fade in the face of—

## SILENCE

# VERSUS

That's what they're all doing, every guest on any late night talk show.

It's not just talking. You have to look between the lines, the laughter, the cue cards and commercial breaks; they do more than talk.

They are on another stage.

They want a piece of your night.

They want a piece of your life.

## DON'T THINK SO?

If you think you're only listening, check back in a half-hour later, while tossing and turning, waging war on the thoughts swirling around in your head, and expect to find at least one of those battle-born thoughts derived from one of the late night talk show discussions.

It's definitely not just talking and being charming or cute.

I am not paranoid. I am not reading into something that shouldn't be read with such scrutiny.

They *are* doing more than talking.

They fight for our attention. They fight for the spotlight.

They fight over-time in hopes that they won't fade with the night.

## ASK YOURSELF

Right before stepping foot on that stage, right before shaking the talk show host's hand, right before you represent your brand, what am I?

## WHAT AM I?

A person.

An old person.

A person that is getting really old.

A person past his prime.

A person that could stand to lose a few pounds.

A person that used to be something but maybe isn't "with it" anymore.

A person that...

## WHAT ARE YOU?

I can't walk that stage. I can't sit down next to that desk, smile and grin and laugh with confidence at the talk show's dry wit.

I can't...

I haven't a clue who I am anymore.

## THEY ARE LAUGHING

They are always laughing. The talk show on mute, I can still hear their laughter. Something was said. The audience is directed to laugh. These aren't laughs; these are confirmations of a celebrity's appeal.

The applause is nothing compared to the expression a laugh brings to the conversation. People put humor before intellect.

Do they want someone to wax intellectual or to tell them a "side-splittingly funny" joke?

I'd want to be honest. I want to be honest with myself.

I would walk that stage, sit in that chair, and tell the wired and tired world that I am lost. Completely lost. I would deviate from the script.

Reason: I'm lost.

Get it?

I would ramble about how you lose yourself in fight to remain relevant to the fans out there. I would ramble about how it's not the other celebrities that end up stealing the spotlight; it's you that steals the spotlight from yourself. You think you have it made but then something about you thinks it can be better. You can make it so much better.

Logic:

## THERE IS MORE
## IT CAN BE BETTER

You fight the fame you've acquired. You think:

The spotlight, it could be so much brighter.

So you change "this," change "that," you become a dizzying league of your own, versions upon versions of yourself fighting to stay interesting.

Ultimately you can't keep up the pace without losing a part.

Remember:

## I'M LOST

There must be a degree of slack given to someone that's so completely lost. I would keep talking about how much is lost in the fight to have it made.

And I'm still not sure I ever got it right.

'James' is getting it right.

He has already mastered the sweet science and he's going to end up being the image attached to the insignia, GREATEST OF ALL TIME.

He will be the G.O.A.T., not me.

Willem Floures, yeah he's that counterpuncher that created a new offshoot of fight psychology where he gets the opponent to fight for him.

There might not even need to be a fight.

He predates "the fight."

He wins before ever stepping in the ring.

## I AM CAUGHT IN THE ROPES

I would ramble for a thousand pages. I would ramble for the entire duration of the interview.

I would derail the entire talk show.

I would be banned from ever returning, my share of the spotlight dimming, limited to anything else but talk shows.

And they'd laugh.

They'd laugh on cue.

They would laugh at me, not at what I'm trying to say.

They would laugh at that too, if they had been listening (they wouldn't). They would laugh at the train wreck I have become.

In that moment, I wouldn't fear for myself; I would fear for the favor I've lost. I'd hope for the best…that maybe they took my diatribe for a sort of performance, a comedic performance.

I would hope that they found it funny.

## DON'T LAUGH

Don't laugh if it's at my expense.

You see, I can't be on these kinds of talk shows. They expect a sort of clever personality that I never had.

I wouldn't even be invited.

The talk show might as well be the place where people judge the person for what they hope to become.

## DON'T LAUGH

I can't stop watching.

One celebrity trips as she walks to her chair. Even that is as intended. Her ditsy persona is flawless. Off camera she is as serious as me but under those bright lights, she can't stop laughing and a minute into the interview, when she looks at the camera, I sense that she is looking at me.

## DON'T LAUGH

She laughs at the fact that I can't look away.

We all know what's about to happen. Yet I can't look away.

The host rolls his eyes. Not amused.

The audience erupts into applause. They are glad to see her leave.

On mute, I read their mouths. The host is saying:

## OUR NEXT GUEST

Like it's directed at me. For a moment I feel foolish.
This isn't about me. Why do I keep turning everything into a problem?
Why do I think everything is some subtle attack on my failing celebrity?

## DON'T LAUGH

I know it's stupid. I know it's really narcissistic but what can a narcissist do to combat the problem? I have no clue. *I didn't used to be this way.*
And then right after I think that I get back to the same confused spiraling logic—

## HOW WOULD I KNOW?

I don't remember.
The talk show host looks right at the camera.
Then looks right at me.
Mouths the words:

LET'S
GET
HIM
OUT
HERE

He walks back to his desk as I walk on stage.

## OH GOD

Where am I?
Isn't this the basement?
What?

It's like I'm here and there. Two places at once.

## THE APPLAUSE

I look so out of place. I am not the brand of celebrity that goes on these kinds of shows. I am not about making these kinds of appearances.

I smile and throw a pitiful little jab in the direction of the audience.

This is humiliating.

It isn't real until the handshake.

Walk over, DON'T trip on the way there, and the host grins in that way that is obviously fake but goes over well with the audience because this is all an act—every moment of it is a gesture of opportunism, nothing else—and he offers the mandatory handshake.

In a mere split second we are shaking hands and it's too late.

Everything goes downhill from there.

## DON'T LAUGH

I'm there but everything is on mute.

I'm here and I've lost the remote again.

The putrid stench of X's dead body blends with the muted terror of the late night talk show into my worst nightmare.

My worst nightmare and I can't be sure it's even mine.

The host asks me a question but I'm too nervous to read his mouth, too nervous to be anything but mute.

He looks into the camera like there's no one there, no one watching, and the reaction he gets makes me sick to my stomach.

There is laughter when I don't respond.

He blames me for the low ratings.

## YOU SHOULDN'T HAVE INVITED ME

## I AM NOT WHAT YOU THINK I AM

## I MIGHT BE THE REAL IMPOSTER

He says something like "Are you or are you not Willem Floures? The fighter?"

We are losing viewers at a rate of ten per minute.

I can do nothing but apologize.

## I AM SORRY

Followed by:

## DON'T LAUGH

This is humiliating.

The host asks me, "So you aren't Willem Floures? The fighter?"

The way he talks down to me doesn't help calm my nerves. I fight back the urge to punch him in the face. I hate how he can't separate the person I am from the reason I am on this talk show.

I can't just be Willem Floures.

I have to be 'Sugar.'

I can't own the name without the alias.

Strip away "the fighter" and I'm no closer to being Willem than you.

## DON'T LAUGH

But they are. They are laughing.

They are all laughing.

The host furrows his brow, "If you aren't Willem Floures, the fighter, then who the hell are you?"

It's the one question I cannot answer and he just asked me. This is why I'm on the show. They want to know why.

Why am I not everything I should be?

Why do I linger around what will only end up making things worse?

Bubbling up from a deep recess of my brain:

## YOU SHOULD RETIRE
## LET HIM GO

## HE DOESN'T WANT TO BE YOU ANYMORE

Talk about myself in the third person, like a mother confronting the source of her son's bad behavior.

You are holding Willem back.

You are a bad influence.

You are out of control.

You tell Willem all of these lies and he thinks they are true.

Willem obeys every single command.

You exploit Willem because you know he'll listen and do everything you say.

You treat Willem like he's a fool.

You tell him all of these lies and you know what he does?

## DON'T LAUGH

Willem tells the world. He shows the world what you've shown him and he does it with pride!

You tell him lies and in return you ruin his credibility.

The world will think he's a joke!

You are the worst thing that's happened to Willem and you need to go.

*You* are the joke.

They will all laugh at you. Willem will be just fine once you let go.

## DON'T LAUGH

But they do. They are laughing.

Everything is muted except for the laughter that sends sickness deeper into my body. It takes every bit of concentration I have to keep it together.

It'll all fall apart.

It's only a matter of time.

## THEY SEE YOU FOR WHO YOU REALLY ARE

The host takes a sip from his mug (it's water, not coffee) and shakes his head. He looks at the audience and asks, "What's that smell?"

It smells awful, I know.

He turns to me, "You smell awful!"

## DON'T LAUGH

But they do. They are laughing.

I smell foul. I smell like a liar.

"I am a liar."

That's all I have to say.

The host's face turns red, "Then who the CENSORED are you?!"

The entire scene washes out not a bright white but rather a sharper sort of contrast. The colors become too overbearing. Every shape and surface becomes too detailed. I feel the knot in my stomach loosen. It loosens and starts climbing up my throat.

The truth is about to come out.

## DON'T LAUGH

I don't know who I am.

## DON'T LAUGH

I cannot explain myself.

## DON'T LAUGH

I am not Willem Floures.

## DON'T LAUGH

Maybe I never was.

## DON'T LAUGH

I am a liar.

## DON'T LAUGH

Every win was really a loss.

## DON'T LAUGH

Every chuckle hurts me to the core.

## DON'T LAUGH

This is humiliating.

## THERE IT GOES

It shoots out of my stomach, spatters all across the host's desk.
Some of it gets on his suit. He stands up slowly, looking at the truth in all its filth. The audience erupts into an uncontrollable laughter.
I couldn't fight back the truth any longer.
I never killed a man.
I never cared about the sick.
I never cared about anyone.
Executioner never disappeared. I kidnapped him.
I betrayed everyone I ever called a friend.
I didn't really win the last fight.
It was rigged.
The truth, it stinks.

## THE LAUGHTER

It singes my eyebrows, leaving only bare skin.
My face warps into a constant gesture of surprise.
The host drops his mug. It shatters as he shouts:

## "GET THIS PIECE OF SHIT OFF MY SHOW!"

It looks bad for everyone involved.

I have never been so humiliated in my life.

Blink twice and I am back in the basement, wondering if any of it happened. I look down at myself. I can't smell the vomit over the stench from X's body. I try to scoop up the lies before they dry but this shirt is ruined.

This also means I'll have to get up from my seat.

I will have to clean myself up.

I will have to take care of X's body.

So be it.

Stand up. Drag the body. Find a burial plot in the back yard. Disregard any onlookers.

The truth is already out there.

## DON'T LAUGH

This ends an era of my existence.

I need to figure out how to save Willem from the onslaught of the media. With X buried, I am next.

'Sugar' has the one fight left.

## HOW AM I GOING TO WIN THIS FIGHT?

I have already lost.

I have already won.

Choose one of the above.

Notice how I begin with the negative. I always see the bad before I see the good. The good thing is that I am able to notice a pattern.

Maybe I am not completely lost.

What I worry about, well what I worry about is obviously a lot, but what I need to worry about right about now is how to pick up the pieces.

I need to find out where they've gone.

What do they have to say about me?

Maybe I can learn more about myself in the process.

I might not survive the revealing but, then again, I didn't think about the long-term consequences of my actions, the "consequences" of having turned every fact into a sort of fiction

just so that I could make myself more interesting for you.
For all of you.

## WONDER

But I do wonder...
What does Willem mean to all of you?

# THE LAUGHTER OF FRIENDS

I want to ask everyone:

## WHAT MAKES YOU LAUGH?

Is it something I did, or was it something I said?

What do you think of me? They whisper into the clouds the nature of their replies. They are nicer than most. They are my friends.

What did you think this was about?

You tried to get an explanation out of me and the best you got was a long diatribe about how I'd be too afraid to be a guest on a talk show.

And yet I still had to make an appearance.

They are friends though.

I have friends just like I had family.

To live in a world is to build up a support network full of friends and family that have your back. Even if you forget to call.

Especially if you lose touch.

They escaped, you know?

## THEY ARE OUT THERE

Fending for Willem.

Willem deserves better.

I bet it's worth a laugh, seeing the damage I've done to the identity.

I was only trying to do what's best for Willem.

Okay, that's a lie. What is one more to add to the pile?

## R.I.P. X

With Executioner buried six feet in the back yard, I sit at the kitchen table. I take ten minutes to face the silence I fear, the silence I drive away with every sort of distraction.

Ten minutes is what I sacrifice in hopes of finding out that I'm not as bad off as I might have remembered.

It takes my full concentration. Focal point is the chair across from me. Don't focus on the clock. Don't focus on the house. Don't focus on yourself.

Keep your focus on something justifiable.

As in:

The chair is a chair.

It is as simple as that. I don't need to wonder if it might be something else. At the very least, I know that the chair across from me is most definitely a chair.

## THE LAUGHTER

In silence, I hear the laughter that scarred me.

It makes these ten minutes a distinct challenge. However, these ten minutes are mine. I face the challenge; I fight back the urge to look away, the urge to listen to my thoughts, and I keep to the chair, my eyes barely blinking:

Focus on the chair.

## WHAT DOES WILLEM MEAN TO YOU?

By now they are on their way.

I return to the basement, return to the seat, return my attention to the TV but not because I need but rather because I "want."

As in: I want to listen.

As in: I want to know what it's like to be Willem Floures in this day and age. I heard it's mostly the same but with a different spin on things.

Counterpuncher is the new knockout artist.

A KO is a cheap fight when a counterpuncher breaks the opponent down until the body winces and the pain is unbearable.

## ESCAPE ARTIST

If you ask me, I'd tell you a story about Willem. It would be from back when the limelight followed me wherever I went. Willem was my name and I was a fighter. Sugar as in sweet science. Sugar as in the alias to end all aliases.

Nothing sweeter than sugar.

I'd sting you with a single shot and you'd be marked.

Nothing personal.

I'm just the better fighter. Even if you weren't sure who was who, I'd let you know how it is in twelve rounds or less. In twelve rounds, you'd meet Willem.

In twelve rounds, you'd meet me.

## SO HOW IS WILLEM DOING?

I admit I hurt his image. Willem Floures is a bit of a joke. According to the media, the moment they found out—lies are lies and lies are fatal—there was a massive pilgrimage towards a competing identity.

Different leagues but do they really have it better?

Willem Floures is a name to remember.

## NOT SO

They didn't seem to think so after I had blurred the line between dignity and humility, honesty and slander. I made it so that no one knew what I'd do next...especially me.

How much of it is imagined?

How much of it is uninspired?

## EXPLAIN YOURSELF

I lean forward, listening to the first interview. They speak to 'Buster' Willem Floures, and the question right about now is the simplest and most difficult to answer:

## WHY SHOULD WE CARE?

Willem Floures captured the world's interest. In order to exist, they will want it to continue. I want to continue. Can I please continue?

This isn't about me; it is only about 'me.'

## WHO ARE YOU VS WHO I AM

Notice the past tense. It's a sad song on repeat, echoing throughout every thought. It makes this all so difficult. I have to listen to them like I'm anyone else. I sit here, television viewer, and it's like the past decades have been unraveled. How much of it is left?

## WHY SHOULD WE CARE?

Friends, why should they care about us? Why should they care about you? Why should they care about Willem?

'Buster' is being interviewed at the gym. He's serious, not a single grin or chuckle at the outlandish questions being asked of him before getting to the all-important one, the one question that'll decide whether or not there is anything to this—anything to him.

"Yeah, so, you had to ask me that question didn't you?"

The interviewer nods, "Our viewers want to know. The state of the league, as it stands, is in tatters after the recent events. We merely look for some sort of understanding. If you are not able to explain yourself, we worry that our time is being wasted."

'Buster' leans on the ropes, casual cool, "I can explain myself. That's on me. So you want the full spiel? Yeah? Well my name is Willem Floures. 'Buster's' my alias. You can call me 'Buster.' I have six wins, zero losses. All six by knockout. I originally moved up here from the South after I heard about how Spencer Mullen's training camp was taking in new recruits. I guess there are a whole lot of us. We all think alike. We're all more or less the same."

He pauses, "What else...?"

The interviewer offers, "Try talking about why you wanted to become a boxer."

Nodding, "Sure. I can talk about that. I don't think I had much of a choice, actually. Fighting followed me. I came from a poor family and I wasn't very popular in school. Growing up I got beat up a lot. I felt like I was getting the sense beaten out of me. I felt like a zero, kind of useless, you know? And so I did my best to do good in school but it wasn't for me. I had okay grades but it wasn't what I had in store. My name was memorable enough so I figured there might be something to it. I ended up choosing boxing instead of basketball and wrestling during junior high. We all got to choose which sport/discipline to study. Boxing was an application. I had to do a lot of soul searching. I had a lot of fight in me. It all clicked together."

Was I poor?

Had I been bullied as a child?

Willem was a natural fighter. I figure most fighters have to get tossed around, beaten up a bit before coming into their own.

A fighter needs to understand what it's like to lose before they can ever achieve a win.

I cringe a little when the interviewer switches to another question, the one about me. 'Me.' 'Sugar.'

Will he tell the world what I did?

"Bad times come and go, you know? I went through a bad time. I felt like I was all tied up inside. I had to reassess my decision to fight. You can't fight if there isn't a deep meaning of why you fight. See—

"Every fight is soul-searching. It is..."

'Buster' searches for the right words before settling with, "The actual dance is the surface. There's a whole 'nother side to a fight."

The interviewer thanks 'Buster' for the tell-all.

I switch channels.

## MY FRIENDS

Do I consider myself a friend?

Do I like myself? Based on what I see next, I get the feeling that I'd be hard to stomach for long periods of time.

Willem Floures is a little self-absorbed.

'Stinger.' That's his alias.

He is invited onto a sports-cast where they discuss and analyze the sports industry at-large.

"Hello Willem, it's nice to have you here," says one of the sportscasters.

"Great to be here," replies 'Stinger.'

"Now, just to make it clear, you are in no way affiliated or a friend to 'Sugar' am I right?"

"That's correct. 'Sugar's' been around a lot longer than I have."

The sportscaster nods, "Right. But I'm sure you are aware of what happened the other night on Late Night, yes?"

"Yes, there's no way I'd forget."

"So it hurt you personally?"

"Why wouldn't it? I took it personal. It's about me."

"I understand," the sportscaster backs off a bit, "it's a lot to handle. Yes…but there have been rumors surrounding 'Sugar's' behavior. I believe it's escalated to widespread online trashing."

'Stinger' looks disappointed, "Yeah, it's taken its toll."

"The widespread belief has to do with a sinister strategy wherein 'Sugar' is said to have concocted the web of deceit to get the upper hand on the entire league. Do you care to comment?"

'Stinger' sighs and I would like to know beforehand what he's about to say but when I try and listen, I only end up hearing stale laughter.

## EXPLAIN YOURSELF

He exhales, "I think it's bullshit. We all do crazy things when we're desperate but I don't think any of his publicity stunts were designed to generate anything other than more publicity skewed in his favor."

"So you are saying that 'Sugar' was only after favor?"

Nodding, 'Stinger' replies, "Yes. That's exactly what I'm saying."

"Interesting…"

Don't say anything about the scars on your wrists. Don't say anything about the scars on your wrists...

"What's that, if you don't mind my asking?"

Shit.

"Oh it's from...night terrors."

I switch channels before I hear anything else.

## EXPLAIN YOURSELF

Oh, wonderful.

In all my channel surfing, I still manage to make it in time for the nightly news. It's about to start.

I kind of hope there's nothing about me but we're not stupid enough to fall back on wishful thinking. All news items deemed "red" will be reported.

It's the nightly news.

They'll probably interview 'James.'

Dynamite.

He'll detonate whatever's left of my dignity to save himself and Willem Floures, boxer celebrity, from facing the scrutiny.

A whole different kind of fight bubbles to the surface.

## IT BEGINS

The intro sequence provides a sample of tonight's top news stories. Among the political are a few celebrity scandals.

Tally of the hopeful (hopeful in that they won't talk about Willem):

Nothing interesting.

Nothing interesting.

Nothing interesting.

Hey look, they discovered a parasite that lives in the human eye.

Nothing interesting.

Looks like Vera Cruz is getting divorced eighteen hours after marrying another guy. That makes for, how many?

Nightly news, don't let me down.

Seven. Seven times married, seven times divorced.

We are all trying our best to remain relevant in a world where media has mistakenly swapped the irrelevant with the relevant.

Nothing interesting.

Nothing interesting.

Sure enough they are interviewing…stomach sinks.

Spencer.

They are interviewing Spencer.

And then two other stories—

## NOTHING INTERESTING

I switch channels out of spite, out of anxiety.

I don't stay on a single channel for any longer than ten seconds. In no time, the channel surfing becomes hypnotic. I fall back into a series of disjointed, self-analytical thoughts as I drift.

As I surf.

## AS IT GOES

The currency of relevancy in the form of broadcast news and entertainment. And there's still the world of social media, where I'm a meme that reads:

## I'LL BE YOU TOMORROW

A picture of me morphed with a sack of sugar. AKA:

A sack of shit.

That's what the bitter world of message boards and the anonymous with too much time on their hands, that's what they think of me.

I'm a sack of sugary shit.

## SUGARMORPH

Another term coined after my late night talk show "cave-in."

It should be harmful but I'm numb.

I don't let it get to me until the repressed emotions become demonic possession: This tired body operating on its own, medicating with painkillers and alcohol, massacring my liver, my mind, my anything, my all.

## EXPLAIN YOURSELF

That's part of the problem.

I did—and look what happened?

I climb from channel two to channel two-hundred all the way back again.

My jaw clenches as I pass by channel four. Nightly News talks about Vera Cruz. There's still time left. The channel surf gets me thinking:

## HOW MANY TIMES WILL I FIGHT BEFORE THE LEAGUE FOLDS?

Willem will be okay right? Beyond 'Dynamite' and the dozen new trainees, there ought to be some assurance that who I have been all my life will more or less live on with the times.

How many times will a fight sell out before the fight identity goes full circle? Do they really want to follow Willem Floures into the next century?

It's a worrisome thought.

I feel responsible for the sensationalism. I should.

I'll deal with it. However, I don't want it to be the one blemish that results in premature extinction of the identity.

## WILLEM FLOURES MUST SURVIVE

Is it time?

When is it not time?

At any given moment, someone is talking about me.

Not me as in all of them. I'm talking about 'me.'

'Sugar.'

By now things are getting bitter.

Okay nightly news…

## HURT MY FEELINGS

I catch the uninteresting story about whatever where one of the representatives wanders around some temple and I get drowsy just thinking about paying attention.

What comes next though…

## THAT WASN'T A QUESTION

Where's "Lights Out" when I need him? That alias ought to mean something. Maybe he's got a power punch to crack a cast-iron chin.

Oh right…

## EXPLAIN YOURSELF

I'm nervous. There. I explained myself.

Spencer has a whole lot more to say though and right from the start the interview proceeds to get under my skin.

The reporter hands Spencer a list of questions, which we see as on-screen graphic overlays, and Spencer proves to be the easiest interview ever for this reporter. Whoever she is.

He starts with a good laugh.

"That's for you," he says, pointing into the camera, and everyone knows he's talking about me.

I feel his laughter echo through me, understanding that it has left an imprint. I will be hearing it again, when silence tries to settle my wired senses.

"And to the world, did you have as good a laugh as I did?"

Spencer smiles, "I hope you did because class is now in session."

Spencer begins his lecture: "I hear all this talk about deceit and the death of Willem Floures from popular culture. I hear all this whining about lies, about sweet gone sour promises. I hear a lot but very little of it has any substance. What I'm not hearing are questions that need to be asked…"

He pauses, waiting for the graphic to appear onscreen.

"I'm not hearing about DYNAMITE VS SUGAR. I don't hear any media buzz surrounding a pivotal fight for Willem Floures."

Spencer slams his fist against open palm.

"This is what we should be talking about! Every identity aches to be heard. Understand? If you want to hear the truth, I'm telling you—save it for fight night. All will be exposed."

## EXPLAIN YOURSELF

There are other questions on that quiz sheet.

I feel like I'm getting off easy. Spencer hasn't answered any questions about me.

No one is talking about 'me.'

Sugar.

My manic episode of media hell.

Why am I being let off so easily?

## EXPLAIN YOURSELVES

I don't care if it affects me because I did what I felt I needed to do at the time. If we rewound these missives, I'd likely end up whining and bragging and contradicting myself until the end of the night.

Nothing would change.

I fought to live.

I live to fight.

The biggest fear of mine is what hinges around judgment. Their laughter burns through my brain, a cast mold representing my time in the ring long since past.

If I'm not fighting, am I dying?

It's irrational but that's what I think about most.

And one other thing:

Willem Floures.

Will they be okay?

Will *he* be okay?

## THEY WILL ALL BE OKAY
## WILLEM WILL BE OKAY

Spencer avoids the questions that needed to be answered. He

coaches the viewers on basic fight psychology.
    He promotes 'James' as the next big thing.
    He's the future.
    I'm the past.
    Together we are Willem Floures.
    Tomorrow, only he will be.
    Me…

## WHERE WILL I HAUNT?

    Don't laugh.
    I just want to keep living after I lose control and the *final fight* is upon me.

# THE LAUGHTER OF FAMILY

I unplug the TV. I've had enough but the feed doesn't want to cease the broadcast. Seems this is important. It continues, the show that isn't really a show, long after the nightly news is over, replacing the late night programming.

There should be infomercials.

Television for insomniacs.

Television for lone viewers.

Television for those of us that have taken one too many punches.

Theoretically speaking, in regards to what I provided above. But everyone wants the truth. It keeps rising up like sickening waves of nausea. I had thought that everything was plain and visible but you see the TV hasn't told the whole story.

What does the TV broadcast when the power is cut?

## SET THE STAGE

How are you feeling?

Are you feeling okay?

I could be better. A lot has happened in the last couple months.

You could say that I'm tired.

We're all tired.

Willem is tired.

## 'ME'

I am tired.

I could get used to the idea of falling asleep, wrapping myself up in bed sheets, for the night rather than waiting until my body gives out. Bed rest like the majority who sleep well because tomorrow is foreseeable. Tomorrow has already been decided. Existence of a routine, a plan, what needs to be done, and none of it has anything to do with you.

You don't need to follow that story.

There is no story to tell. It's a dry spell. Mundane.

## THEN LET THEM SPEAK

I'm listening.

That's what this is ultimately about, right?

*Him.*

Willem Floures.

I'd like to believe that I know the guy, but it seems they got a better idea than anything I might have had, once upon a time.

## ONCE UPON A TIME

Okay, scratch that.

Drop the "once upon a time." It ages me significantly.

## I WATCH
## I LINGER

On the TV disconnected, the TV unplugged, I see a blank stage.

It's a blank stage and it knows that it's a blank stage. Graphic overlay states the obvious:

## BLANK STAGE

Duh.

The graphic changes to—

## BLANK SLATE

And part of me has already moved on. The part that remains is 'Sugar' and all that I hold back, every little bit of the lies that

I have yet to fully expose. If I wanted to I would. If I needed to I would blurt it out.

## DON'T DO IT

I don't intend on saying a thing.

I wouldn't want people to hear me talking to myself, right?

The blank stage is a blank slate that I can barely see given the lack of a light source. You can just barely see it and if I squint my eyes, a light flickers on, illuminating the stage.

The light gets brighter as I lean back, unsure of what to expect.

The bright empty stage washes white and pulls back to reveal four red recliners, complete with the impression that with a single shiver, a single sigh, the scene will evolve to include an opening statement.

What happens when I hold my breath?

## DON'T DO IT

Why? Will I suffocate?

Can that even happen—can a person really die by holding their breath?

I exhale when I see what holding my breath does to the scene onscreen. Seems like that's a no. You can't die by holding your breath but you can inspire a title sequence complete with music that causes the basement where you linger to rumble from the foundation to the rhythm of the theme song.

It's a familiar song.

It's my entrance music.

Death growls mixed with down-tuned drop-C guitar.

Scrolling across the screen are the names of would-be aliases, fighters looking for a fight, boxing professionals looking to be featured:

'Cobra'

'Storm'

'Jersey Devil'

'Kid Perfect'

Four for the price of one moment of saddening humiliation.

Rubbing your eyes reveals shapes sitting in those red recliners and proceeding to avoid rubbing your eyes in hopes that the shapes will not turn into four people, mirror images of the one likeness that should be extremely familiar only results in the instantaneous crescendo of the broadcast bringing up the title of the show:

## WE NEED TO TALK TO YOU

And the subtitle:

## IS THERE A FUTURE FOR WILLEM?

Hold back as much as you want but I can't help but bring them to fruition, four young fighters, four young aliases, four of me that have yet to be, but will begin fighting their way up the league ladder in the months and years that outlast 'me.'

If there was ever any other version of me it was 'me,' or who I am after losing the alias that I popularized and then pulverized with lies.

'_____'

## OR WITHOUT SUGAR

They wear expensive suits from my closet and they sip from the last four coffee mugs I used. They are replicas of the four best moments of my prime years; they represent four different styles of boxing:

## BRAWLER

## BOXER-PUNCHER

## COUNTERPUNCHER

## SWARMER

If you try to figure out who's who, it only makes them look

right at you. Right at me. Right at the camera and right into my eyes, like the screen doesn't separate us. Anything I do to look away only helps further define their broadcast. They aren't talking but I have to start worrying.

I just have to think about myself in a manner that is extremely selfish.

I just have to bring up the thought, "I am not that old…"

It gives them voice.

It gives them my voice.

## DON'T DO IT

"Tonight we have a lot to cover," one of them says (I haven't a clue who because thankfully they haven't yet introduced themselves).

I listen and that gives them the right to do exactly what I dread.

The one talking points to the one on the far right, "Why don't we get the introductions out of the way?"

And just like that, an "alias," they exist:

WILLEM 'JERSEY DEVIL' FLOURES
BOXER-PUNCHER

'STORM' WILLEM FLOURES
SWARMER

WILLEM 'KID PERFECT' FLOURES
COUNTERPUNCHER

'COBRA' WILLEM FLOURES
BRAWLER

'Kid Perfect' plays host because he's the one that'll fight first out of the four of them. Why the number four? But I stop that thread before it can be more than a partial thought, fearing that it might give rise to a fifth.

## DON'T DO IT

I'm not. I took care of it.

'Kid Perfect' nods, "It's great to be here. The nature of our debate and subsequent discussion pertains to whether or not we will fight at all:"

Superimposed onto the screen right as he says it:

## IS THERE A FUTURE FOR WILLEM?

"We need to think about him, not for what he has become but rather for what he might *be*. As an athlete and surely a fan of the entire league, I cannot stand to see my name dragged through the filth. I have seen 'Sugar' do some really great things but I…I just can't let him insult me the way he has."

Cringe but I lean forward, tuned in.

Captivated. Being captivated means I care. Caring means I have that voice lingering louder, the voice that carries the laughter.

## DON'T DO IT

I guess it's too late, now that you're here.

I see you there. He stands in the back.

'Black Mamba' complete with every bruise, cut, and blemish that had been my beat-the-shit-up body a fight ago.

He stands in the back, watching me, not the other four. They might as well not even be there. 'Black Mamba' mouths the words:

## DON'T DO IT

And the three words form and fit every possible worry I might have.

Worries include:

Will any of them beat my record?

Will any of them conclude what will be made true by the end of this chapter? For that matter, will any of them be the one that provokes me into…

## DON'T DO IT

…into 'doing,' as in saying, as in assuming that it has to be said?

Surely it's possible. My record isn't what it used to be. Every loss counts for five wins. If you lose, you better win your next five.

Every win is, at best, fifteen seconds in the limelight.

I had my fifteen before it faded and, not only that: the media logged Willem for unwarranted attention.

It hurts me but it hurts them too.

'Cobra' speaks up, "I agree. Willem is no longer a name that brings the kind of attention and respect we want as we begin our careers. Willem is a sideshow freak compared to the other names, those leagues that are doing quite well."

'Storm' adds, "Last Devon Morris event sold out."

'Kid Perfect' sighs, "That has never ever happened before. Morris is nowhere near as good as me."

"Right," 'Jersey Devil' says, "and it's all because of the favor being lost. It's dripping away like an open wound."

'Kid Perfect' fields the next opportunity to blame me, "Willem holds records for longest boxing win streak, quickest jab, and best boxing performance eight years in a row but—"

## BUT…

Here they go—

"But with a single promotional campaign, 'Sugar' flatlined all interest."

"But within two fights he changed the world's opinion."

"But with one campaign he went against all principles of persona."

"But with one campaign he confused all understanding."

Doesn't really matter who said what, does it?

I don't exactly hold myself up to being a good person. If you had to ask me at this very moment what I think of myself, in terms of an entity, as something alive, as something that exists, I will say that I am a person.

I think.

Something tugs at the thread of thought that becomes a single sentence that repeats over and over but I can't hear it because the laughter 'Black Mamba' lets boil to the surface drowns it out so that it's white noise.

You and I—

We've figured out what needs to be done.

However, I still hold back to dead scraps.

Hey X, what do you think?

But no, he's dead.

That part of me is dead.

'Black Mamba' wants me to keep my mouth shut.

## DON'T DO IT

No matter what they say and do to provoke me.

No matter what is said to diminish my contribution, my boxing legacy.

But then I get to thinking about how they'll simply blame it on 'me.'

*'Sugar' was a blemish was a bad particular era for boxing.*

## I WATCH
## I LINGER

I see it in their faces. It's what I would do to survive.

Unanimous agreement—

"Anything that intends on surviving must fight to win!"

The future intends on rendering my era as a blemish and nothing more. But I'm afraid I can't do that.

'Black Mamba' shakes his head, eyes bulging, dark tar-like blood dripping from his nose:

## NO

But I'm smarter than that. I have, at the very least, learned one thing about myself. Willem is a coward, a self-conscious individual incapable of simply taking a risk; I can't just "do something" without coming up with alternatives, a weigh-in of what can and will occur.

What might go wrong?

As in, hey 'Black Mamba' what can go wrong?

## DON'T DO IT

That's all he can say because it's the fear talking.

It's the fear that I've held onto; it's the fear that continually pervades my decisions. I keep thinking about what I'll lose and have prevented a number of pivotal career decisions from coming to fruition because I simply couldn't have let things evolve on their own.

Like that one time I…

## SNAP PUNCH
## OR THE PUNCH THAT COULD HAVE BEEN

It's a punch that Spencer is likely teaching 'James' to later implement in future fights (look out for that guys—it's a killer).

He tried to teach me as he's tried so many times but I really fought against his tutelage. He explained how it should be done but I doubted him.

Besides, it was all on paper. Nothing about the punch worked without developing it from the foundations of the uppercut.

So the snap punch, according to Spencer, is a powerful split-second switch-up that can be moved into from both straight and hook punches.

The beauty of the punch is how you don't have to be in any particular situation; your footwork could be shaky. You could be winded and playing defensive in order to go the distance.

Maybe you're playing the fight to its final moments and doing that usually means playing it real safe.

## DON'T DO IT

Exactly, 'Black Mamba.'

What I used to do all the time.

Well, anyway, back to the punch. It involves utilizing the same principle of throwing an overhand punch (shoulders tilted, arm arching out, sitting down on the punch fully, hips and all) but in using it, the "snap punch" evolves instantly (like a "snap") from a preexisting punch.

You morph into it.

It's complicated and requires a lot of practice.

I listened to the fear.

## DON'T DO IT

And I wonder if that's the reason why I have a good "chin."

Maybe it's not that I took punches but rather because I backpedaled and played defensive games to avoid punches.

Frankly it didn't take much to send me to the canvas.

Right X?

## I WATCH

I move my chair right up to the TV.

I press my face right up to the screen so that my forehead feels the warmth and the cartilage of my nose (broke it three times over the course of my career, just saying) bends just enough to hear that all-too-familiar crack. The sound of age. But I'm not here to deny it. I am here to:

## LINGER

And watch as 'Black Mamba' fades from the stage.

Not that I don't deny the fear. It's just that I need to go through with it. I need to say it. I need to admit it.

To myself.

I need to make it so that they can't devalue my era.

'Me.'

I will be remembered.

"We can do better than this," says 'Storm.'

They are all in agreement about what to do to survive.

They need to fight. They need to fight me. Victory would be to send Willem into a second chance sort of scenario where I am scapegoat.

If I am unwilling to admit to my exploitation, they are more able to align with every single part of me that I've kidnapped, wounded, and ignored.

If I still hold back, I will give into the fear.

I will lose the biggest fight of all.

## IT ALL DISAPPEARS…
## UNLESS

I don't want that to happen. So I let the laughter swarm in as I press my lips against the screen. I lick the screen in one long upwards motion.

The eager, would-be parts of me shut up, turn and look right at me.

## DO I GET YOUR ATTENTION?

Silence.

## GOOD

Four sets of eyes watching borders on the sensation that I'm finally reaching the first stages of understanding.

Forget about the whole spiritual side to this; I basically feel like I'm getting at something. I'm beginning to figure out how it all fits together.

*Beginning*, the key word. It seems I will have to let the other parts of me, all of them, work on figuring the *middle* and the *end*.

But check it out:

In the blink of an eye I send the KO punch that eliminates any possibility of their eradication of my era. In sports history, my records hold true. In sports history, I am 'Sugar' Willem Floures.

I tell-all like the ones that escaped me:

I KNOW THAT IT'S MY FAULT

I KNOW THAT I FELL INTO SOUR TIMES

WE ALL FIGHT OURSELVES FOR SO LONG WE
FORGET WHICH BOUNDARIES NOT TO CROSS

I RUINED THINGS BUT I ALSO RESTORED THE
URGENCY TO THE ENTIRE SPORT, TO THE REASON
WHY I FOUGHT AT ALL

I FOUGHT TO UNDERSTAND

I FOUGHT TO BE FOUND

AND YOU KNOW WHAT?
I DID

WILLEM FLOURES IS NOTHING TO LAUGH ABOUT

# THE LAUGHTER OF STRANGERS

Build up the laughter so loud that it drives me out of the basement. I leave the empty crowd of my thoughts back where they should remain hidden:

At ringside.

I ascend those old wooden steps and realize that it's morning. Another night driven away like a lost opportunity. I listen to the house creak in line with the rise and fall of my breath. I tune into my surroundings, listening to the laughter disappear as I shut the basement door.

In the silence, I am not held back by the worry, the fear.

I am left with the one thought that I feel needs to be asked:

## WHAT DOES A STRANGER SEE?

Look at me and what do you see?

If you asked me I'd say that I'm at the very least a person. I mentioned that before so I don't need to get back into that. Besides, I'm not a stranger. It defeats the purpose of the query.

If I introduced myself to a stranger, someone that had no clue who I was, what would they think?

Would they see any redeeming qualities?

Or would I just be another sad sack of bruised, scarred, tattooed flesh?

## I WONDER

I wonder how I weigh in, and I'm not talking about weight class and boxing. I wonder how I weigh in as a person.

## I AM A PERSON

But that isn't saying much if I can't describe who that person is beyond the fact that "he" lives and breathes. Spencer must have seen something in me because he continues to train me into what he hopes will be the best fighter ever. A real G.O.A.T candidate.

Too bad then…

Too bad that I won't be the one to do it.

I am not the Greatest of All Time.

Current status:

## LOST OPPORTUNITY

One too many bad decisions kind of dismisses you from the candidacy.

But I admit it.

I take that from them.

I took and took some more and left behind the groundwork that'll make Willem a better fighter and, who knows, maybe even a better person.

But what does a stranger see?

## WHERE DOES A STRANGER GO?

Where do I go from here? How will my final fight end?

I listen to the footsteps that are mine to follow. I follow those footsteps into the dining room, a room that is barely ever used. I draw lines across the dusty surface of the table. I follow the footsteps to the expensive silverware.

I pick up a silver plate and look at my reflection.

## THIS IS WHAT A STRANGER SEES

I inspect the right side of my face, which hasn't healed as well as before. I look like I have been in quite a few fights. To a stranger, I look like I've lived a rough life. Tough times for the one that hopes to find something memorable to keep them from anonymity.

I grip the plate and toss it against the wall.
It doesn't break, the silver resonating a dull sound.

## WHAT DOES A STRANGER THINK?

I follow the footsteps around to the room where I used to watch most fights with Spencer. The TV flickers on, just to point me in the direction of where I need to look, where I hope to find.
On the TV, I see the words:

## I DON'T THINK WE'VE MET

And I take three steps forward, not four, standing where the footsteps have stopped.
I speak to the TV like it's a person.
I say, "Hello, my name is—"
But what is my name?
I hesitate until the name is said for me, the screen flickering the response:

## WILLEM FLOURES, RIGHT?

"Right," I nod.
First impressions are everything. I think of what to say to make this introduction worthwhile and interesting.
The TV flickers:

## NICE TO MEET YOU

And I reply, "You too. I'm so glad to meet you."
I hear the tapping of a footstep, signal that this is running long. I need to say something. Anxiety. What do you tell a stranger that doesn't seem obvious, that doesn't sound like I'm trying too hard?
TV flicker.

## WHAT DO YOU DO?

It's always the next question after "name" huh?

I very well can't say fighter because then it'll be about what kind of fighter, weight class, and everything I've already left behind, down in the basement, with the laughter.

So I say, "I'm an athlete."

### REALLY, LIKE A PROFESSIONAL ATHLETE?
### WHAT SPORT?

I can't get away from it.
The identity that is mine. But don't get me wrong—
I believe what I said before, said to them:
I admit it. "I admit it."
I smile, "I'm a bit of a fighter."

### FIGHTER, LIKE MIXED MARTIAL ARTS?

More traditional, more pure than that.
"Boxing."
TV flicker.

### WAIT A MINUTE...

And see how now we aren't strangers anymore? This is not about what a stranger sees. The stranger ultimately figures out who I am, and that's something to consider. I consider the fact that I can't get past who I was; it is a part of me now. Willem will go on without me but part of Willem remains with me. I am Willem, after all.

TV flicker.

### I'VE SEEN SOME OF YOUR FIGHTS
### YOU ARE A GREAT FIGHTER

"Thank you."
The footsteps move on. The TV flickers one last time.

### WELL IT WAS REALLY NICE TO MEET YOU!

I follow the footsteps out of the room and into the foyer.

I realize that I am too. I'm glad to have met...

Past tense: To have been able to meet someone.

Present and Future: To be able to meet anybody.

The footsteps lead me upstairs and to the one room that matters. The one room that usually has its door closed.

The footsteps continue into the room but I need to get past the door. I knock, "Sarah?"

No answer.

I try again, to no avail.

I try the door, mildly surprised to see that it's unlocked, and I hesitantly wander into the room.

I remember:

## THE LAST TIME I WAS IN HERE I FOUND OUT MY TIME IN THE SPOTLIGHT WAS OVER

I see that Sarah is missing. Well, maybe not missing but she's definitely not in her room. I momentarily wonder about whether or not this is the right room and whether or not the other rooms are replicas of Sarah's room.

I have never been in any of the other upstairs bedrooms.

I have only ever populated the basement and first floor of the house.

The footsteps direct me to a dollhouse in the corner of the room. I wander over and look inside. A few dolls sit around a table while one doll is lying down on a bed in one of the dollhouse's upstairs rooms.

I take the doll that I assume is the father and the doll that I assume is the older son, both the same brand of doll, identical save for the different shirts, and I hold them up to my face.

I look into the face of the inanimate object.

The doll appears to be happy.

What about the other?

Same.

## WHAT DOES A STRANGER SEE?

I see that they are content being dolls.
They suit their purpose.

## NOW THE OTHER WAY AROUND

What do they see in me?
Am I the fighter I should have been? I did my best. I had some great fights. I repeat this, speaking to the dolls, "I did my best. I had some great fights…" I stop and look around the room, checking the closet just to make sure Sarah isn't there. I don't want her to see me playing with the dolls.

## WHY DOES THAT MATTER?

It matters.
It doesn't matter.
I don't know. Anyway—
"I'd like to think that I come off as a nice guy. I might look a little scary due to the tattoos, the scars, and the fact that I have trouble smiling due to nerve damage to my face." It's a lie but a good one to use when people start wondering why you're so serious all the time; besides, if I repeat that enough I might believe it and then it exists. It becomes something somewhat interesting, something memorable at least for the strangers to hear about upon first introduction.

## WHAT DO YOU DO?

I know what they do. They "exist" as toys for tots, for young kids; they are dolls. That's about as simple a description as it can get.
"I am an athlete."

## REALLY, LIKE A PROFESSIONAL ATHLETE? WHAT SPORT?

"Boxing."

# WOW. WHAT'S IT LIKE TO BE IN THE RING? IN A FIGHT?

I follow the footsteps to the bed.

I create an imaginary ring out of a pillow and I sit among the two dolls, each representing one corner.

## WHAT DOES A STRANGER SEE?

In a perfect fight, there has to be a reason, deeply rooted beyond victory and loss. You have to fight for personal reasons.

You have to fight knowing that this is an expression of who you are, the strength that lies within ready to be tested, ready to surface in the form of a flurry of fists. Fisticuffs.

The stranger watching a fight sees it as more or less an act of gladiatorial combat. Our modern society is witness to fight nights brimming with the underlying representation of just how amazing the human body truly is—

It is versatile and can go the distance.

It can give, and take, more punishment than we could ever imagine.

The human mind is the real problem. It is the one influence that can turn the perfect fight into a planning exercise.

I wonder:

## WHAT MIGHT A PERFECT FIGHT BE?

It goes the distance. That's for sure.

I want it to be a barnburner. Both fighters compliment each other in terms of fighting style. They fight with the intention of a knockout but they simply fail to do so.

I put myself into the equation.

What would it take to deliver the perfect fight?

## THE PERFECT FIGHT

It seems like something I should really consider. So, okay, let's think about this. Doll one is 'me' and let's make doll two 'James.'

Fight prediction:

## 'SUGAR' VS 'DYNAMITE'

Will it be a perfect fight?

I'm a boxer-puncher which means I can go both ways, offense and defense; he's a counterpuncher which means he'll attempt to keep me on the offensive by being so defensive.

I exhale because it's a bit warm in the house.

The air conditioning turns on as the last bit of air escapes my lungs.

More comfortable now, I begin my round-by-round prediction.

Addressed to the stranger, this is, in my humble opinion, the perfect fight.

## ROUND ONE

We feel each other out—the first thing any boxer does is figure out the rhythm of his opponent. I lead with the jab while 'James' leans and warms up with some fancy evasive footwork. I win this round because of the jab.

'James' barely lands any more than a dozen punches.

## ROUND TWO

'James' figures out my fight rhythm. He knows that I'll switch from right to southpaw when I want to land powershots. He keeps on the defensive and I will become quite frustrated if I don't do something to keep this from happening but it doesn't happen in this round.

'James' wins the round based on number of punches landed. Most of mine are jabs and hooks to the body, which 'James' brushes off with countering hooks of his own to my face, which I leave wide open.

## ROUND THREE

I lead with straights to the face. 'James' feels the pressure from consistent left straights to the face. He defends against most but the sudden pressure keeps him slightly confused.

This is unexpected.

I have to rely on the unexpected. The score is close, real close.

'James' stays competitive with an uppercut landed perfectly, which stuns me a minute left in the round.

Continue to apply pressure.

I win the round, just barely.

## ROUND FOUR

The previous round was really close so I get a little anxious. Of course I get anxious. That's exactly what 'James' wants. This is where he sends me to the canvas, knockdown number one of five.

For it to be a perfect fight, I feel it's necessary to include the number five.

I get back up after the three count. My right knee touched the canvas. It's a flash knockdown using a textbook counterpunch to my one-two jab combination (neither punch landed).

'James' doesn't capitalize on the knockdown.

We keep trading punches. I trade not because it's smart but because it makes a statement to the strangers in the crowd, the thousands, the millions watching:

I am not afraid.

I am not afraid of his clear skill and edge in both power and age. I will fight this fight like we both die by round twelve. Nothing to lose.

Though his footwork overshadows mine, I weave in and out of a four-punch flurry at the end of the round that unsettles 'James.'

He wins the round because of the knockdown but I watch him between rounds, shaking my head as if to say—

You have to do better than that. I'm going to touch the canvas every damn round. I'm not staying down. You'll have to punch me to death if you intend on the win being by KO.

I have been KOed too many times.

This fight, the perfect fight, is not one where I lose by knockout.

Between round four and five Spencer shouts, loud enough for everyone at ringside to hear, about what needs to change.

YOU ARE NOT GOING TO HURT HIM!
YOU ARE NOT GOING TO HURT HIM!

No. You won't.

I know what hurts me and what doesn't.

I know about fear and I've faced it.

This is the aftermath, the result.

'James,' you get to be the last person that fights me.

It's a privilege you'll regret later.

ROUND FIVE

'Spencer's' words confuse 'James' and I capitalize by throwing weak flurries of jabs and straights to the face.

He defends but cannot seem to fall back into his groove.

I win the round up until he lands a hook to my stomach, knocking me down to the canvas.

Two of five.

I get back up by the five count and I send my own uppercut, which I had intended on being the "snap punch" I told you about, but it doesn't work.

The uppercut, though, sends him to his knees for a fraction of a second, enough for the referee to slip between the both of us, calling it a knockdown.

It's one of those kinds of knockdowns that really isn't a knockdown but the referee starts counting anyway.

Spencer is pissed and I get a sick thrill out of hearing him shout.

I don't have a corner in this fight, only the cutman I paid and the two others who make sure I stay hydrated and awake.

In this fight, I am my own trainer.

It's a draw.

The round is split down the middle, some favoring 'James' some favoring 'me.'

## ROUND SIX

I take the round off, being as defensive as I can.

I'm old. I can't go the distance without taking at least one round off.

I show the world that I have a great defense. More importantly, I show 'James' that I can be defensive too.

A boxer-puncher is the real wildcard.

Remember that.

Cocky and confident until he sends me down to the canvas with the same uppercut.

Three of five.

I get up after the five count. I'm fine but the referee whispers in my ear, "You get knocked down again and I'll be forced to stop the fight."

He won't stop the fight.

Empty threat.

'James' wins the round.

## ROUND SEVEN

I win this round. 'James' doesn't take the round off; I steal the round from him. We trade punches for three-fourths of the round. He hits me with a great hook that nearly takes the wind out of me but I counter with a hook to the side of his face. It scares him. Proof that he's a young fighter:

The blind shots cultivate fear.

I'd say that the majority of shots that hurt me are the ones I can see coming but cannot evade. Blind shots are convenient blackouts.

I wish I could get a punch to the face every night. Maybe then I'd be able to sleep. That is, if it wasn't unhealthy to take knockout-inducing shots to the face every night. Anyway—

The last ten seconds are mine.

'James' knows that he'll win if he knocks me down again so he becomes a bit predictable. I use that as an opportunity to crack his "perfect" defense.

It starts with two blocked jabs but then I send an uppercut, same uppercut he's used against me all throughout the fight, and it causes him to drop his gloves. Arms at his sides, stunned, cracked, I send eight shots to the stomach followed by another uppercut to the chin, before he can bring himself to defend again. Bell, end of round.

My round not his.

## ROUND EIGHT

It's bad for me but I expect it going in.

Spencer motivates 'James' into taking me out this round.

### YOU GOT TO END IT NOW.
### NOT NEXT ROUND. NOW!

And he tries.

He really tries.

Four of five—

To the canvas I go, same uppercut. The referee brings the fight doctor out due to the cut just under my right eyebrow.

Blood drips into my eye.

The doctor says that I'm okay.

I narrowly evade having the fight end but the round is obviously 'James's.'

## ROUND NINE

I have trouble seeing due to the cut but I take the round using sheer force. I fight southpaw the entire round just to aggravate 'James.'

Mostly jabs and cheap shots to the body.

'James' spends most of the round silent and defending. Fighting southpaw confuses him into slowing down.

He'll get a talking to from Spencer that's for sure.

My round.

## ROUND TEN

I intentionally fight dirty. I need to take another round off, getting pretty gassed. People can tell. The referee is beyond worried.

I let him have this round but I let him know that he can't hurt me by clinching whenever he attempts more than a single punch.

The crowd boos a little, but even the perfect fight has a number of highs and lows.

This is a tough round to judge.

I get in cheap kidney shots when we clinch.

I bring him to the ropes and fight using rope-a-dope, using the ropes to prop me up as I lean back and launch forward with extra force single jabs to his face. Most of the round, I punch not to the body or face but to his gloves.

I do it because no one does it.

I win the round.

The round I took off to rest.

## ROUND ELEVEN

It's bad. The cut gets worse despite what the cutman does to keep it from getting bigger. 'James' focuses on the cut and by the end of the round I am nearly dead on my feet, blood down my chest, the front of his shorts stained with my blood.

His round. No doubt about it.

This went the distance and physically we both have to pay for it.

## ROUND TWELVE

He knocks me down at the beginning. Uppercut.

Five of five.

The referee counts instead of calling it.

I get to eight before standing up.

He looks into my eyes and says, "I'm going to let you fight because you got this far. Don't make me regret it!"

And I don't. I let fists fly. I dig deep into the tank.

I leave nothing for tomorrow.

This is my last.

His defense avoids eighty percent of my onslaught but everyone is shocked to see the elder of the two fighters taking the last round.

He'll win the round because he knocked me down, but I win the fight in terms of psychology.

I silence him in the last and as the bell rings, I know that I've lost. I needed to lose in order for Willem to rise back to the top.

But even in losing, I know what just happened.

"It is, it really is."

There you have it, the perfect fight.

In my humble opinion, there is no greater fight I can give.

This is my best performance.

In my best performance, I lose.

You can laugh if you want, strangers.

The laughter of a stranger is not always bad. It gets old and loses all meaning. So let them laugh. It won't always hurt this bad.

You can wash it in the sorrows that bleed the same bright white from before, but this time it all seems so new when you're empty handed.

No longer holding onto much of anything.

Just your face, looking back at you in the mirror, waiting to be redefined. Waiting for a description.

We know what a stranger sees…

BUT WHAT ABOUT YOU? WHAT DO YOU SEE?

# THE SILENCE

In the silence of the bedroom, I hear myself talking. Not 'myself' but myself—who I am now. In the silence, I hear myself saying, "Hey, how are you feeling?" That's a question I'd ask someone that's gone twelve rounds but that would mean I can't be talking to myself because I have twelve rounds to go.

## LAST FIGHT

Alongside my last fight there will be a series of lasts—
Last chance to make things right.
Last statement before receding into the world of anonymity. The public doesn't look for sound bites or blurbs from the fold of people you call life. They look for the notable identities to buoy whatever it is they are trying to sell.
I hear myself talking, and it sounds like me.
It sounds like what I imagined I'd sound like.
It's not that far off from anything you'd hear Willem saying.

## THAT'S BECAUSE

"I know, I know."

## YOU REALLY NEED TO START GETTING USED TO

"Yes, I know."

## YOU SHOULDN'T INTERRUPT PEOPLE
## WHEN THEY ARE

"Yes, I know."

## SEE? THAT'S YOUR PROBLEM

"Yeah and what's my problem?"

## YOU THINK YOU KNOW EVERYTHING

I laugh, "I assure you that I don't have that problem. If anything, I know how to make toast and survive in a fight. Not much else. Wait. No. I got something else. I have ten toes and nine-and-a-half fingers. I lost that tip of my left pinky finger during that, you know…"

## I KNOW

"Of course you know because—"
"What are you doing?"
A voice that could only be Sarah's.
"Oh, hey Sarah." Looking down at the two dolls in my hands, recalling instantly how odd this must look, dolls, talking to myself, in her room when I'm not supposed to be, "I was… wondering where you went."
She wanders over, takes one of the dolls from me and says, "You shouldn't be in here!"
Her tone is scolding more so than angry.
"Yeah, sorry. I was just following the—"

## YOU SOUND LIKE A LUNATIC

"Never mind."
She looks at her doll, "What were you doing in here?"
Doing my best to change the topic of conversation, I ask, "What were you doing out of your room?"
She places both hands on her hips, "What am I, some kind of prisoner?!"
I shake my head, "No, no, just…I don't know."
"Of course you don't know!"

## SMOOTH, REAL SMOOTH

What else am I going to do? I relent, "Yeah you're right."

She exhales deeply, the house shaking at the peak of the sigh, "Whatever…"

I remain seated on the edge of the bed as Sarah wanders over to the mirror and, unsurprisingly, she lacks a reflection.

## YOU DON'T FIND IT ODD?

I am the only person within frame.

She turns and looks at me, "What?"

"Nothing."

"It's not nothing. What?"

"It's just…"

She returns her attention to the mirror, "Oh, this."

## YOU ALREADY KNOW WHAT SHE IS, DON'T BOTHER

"You are probably wondering what it means for you."

I admit that, yes, it's a little selfish but…

## DON'T SAY ANYTHING

She sets the doll down on the end table next to me.

"You see me right?"

I nod.

"That's only because you know my dad. You know my name."

"Yeah."

"I don't exist to the world out there. This is how we are."

Looks at me, "Get it?"

## YES YOU DO

"You mean…"

## OH JESUS

"What don't you understand?"

I hold up the doll, "By 'we' do you mean 'us,'" referring to the inanimate doll, "or 'us,'" pointing to the room as a whole, meaning all the hauntings within the house.

"I mean 'us' as in everyone that watches the media. Everyone that watches one of your fights. Everyone that—"

"Laughs..."

## THERE YOU GO INTERRUPTING PEOPLE AGAIN

She nods, "Right."

For a while we are silent, sitting there thinking about all of this while Sarah brushes her hair. When she's done doing that, she wanders over to her dollhouse, takes the one I'm still holding, and puts them back in position.

She sits next to the dollhouse, facing the opposite side.

"Why are you sitting there? You can't see into the house that way."

"Yeah I can. I see from the outside looking in. I see into the house the way anyone else would if they really wanted to look."

## SILENCE

We sit in silence. I resist talking to myself until the words seemingly escape me like they did:

## RIGHT ABOUT NOW IT HAS STARTED

## RIGHT ABOUT NOW IT'S THE BEGINNING OF THE END

Sarah isn't put off by this, "How is the fight going?"

I shrug, "It's still round one. Feeling each other out."

Realizing how odd this is, I narrow my eyes, "How do you know?"

She makes a face, "My dad is at the fight, duh."

## DUH!

"You are very mature for your age, you know that?"

"I have to be."

"Who takes care of you anyway?"

She looks into one of the dollhouse windows, "I take care of myself."

"'James' used to right?"

She shakes her head, "I took care of 'James.'"

"What?"

"Dad wanted someone to watch 'James' just in case."

## JUST IN CASE

"Just in case I..."

She nods, "Yeah. You tend to lose track of yourself."

"Yeah, but everyone changes, right? Everyone doesn't stay the same like we maybe want to. I know the media wants the same from someone when it's good but that just doesn't happen."

She turns the dollhouse around, "Yeah."

"So you agree?"

## WHAT DO YOU CARE?

"Yeah," she grabs one of the female dolls, "I agree."

Sarah stands up and walks back to the mirror.

She brushes the doll's hair.

## THE SILENCE

She asks again, "How's the fight going?"

"It's going well. Round three. I am pressuring 'James' with straight shots to the face. The judges and commentators seem a bit surprised that I am able to take some of the momentum of the fight away from 'James.'"

She nods, "Yeah."

## THE SILENCE

I ask her, "You already know all this, don't you?"

She turns, looks at me, a straight face, and returns to the combing of the doll's hair.

I don't know what that means.

## YES YOU DO

No I don't.

But okay, let's change the subject.

To what? Umm…

"So…"

Sarah interrupts, "Are you actually going to get knocked down five times?"

## YEAH

"Yeah."

"That's unheard of."

I shrug, "It's my last fight and—"

"And you want to make it perfect."

## WHAT IS WITH ALL THE INTERRUPTIONS?

"Yeah. I was going to say 'good' but perfect is better."

Sarah replies, "Perfect is the right choice."

I have to ask…

"You are going to ask about my dad right?"

"Yeah."

"Go ahead and ask."

## YES, GO AHEAD AND ASK

"Does he think I'll be remembered?"

## WRONG QUESTION

Sarah sighs, "What's the question?"

I reconsider, opting for something simpler:
"What does Spencer think of me?"

REALLY?

Sarah doesn't say anything until she returns to the dollhouse and rearranges the layout.
The house shakes.

DOES SHE REALLY HAVE TO KEEP DOING THAT?

Doing what?

CHANGING THE WAY THINGS ARE

"Yeah," Sarah says, "change is good."

THE SILENCE

We are silent for some time. I watch Sarah reconfigure the entire dollhouse. The house sounds like it's about to collapse. I cringe but hold back, choosing to imagine the silence I used to loathe.
"How is it that you are able to predict what I'm about to say?"
She laughs, "You're not serious are you?"
Umm.
"Oh, you are." Sarah laughs, "You are talking to yourself and you don't even realize it! That's a really bad habit."
"I am?"
"It's really bad, yeah. It's bad because you don't realize that you're having a separate conversation with yourself."
"Yeah…"
"Like there's a whole group of people, an entire audience, listening to your every word or something."
Sarah can't stop laughing.
"I admit it's bad but can you please stop laughing?"
"Oh," she clears her throat, "sorry. But I guess you're used to being in the spotlight. Dad always said you treated everything

like it was on camera." She moves around one room and attaches it to the attic.

It's this room.

The entire room shakes violently. For one brief moment, I watch as one of the windows looks like it's about to shatter.

But doesn't.

"It's okay," Sarah says, "I do this all the time."

"Why do you change everything around?"

"I like the challenge." She turns the dollhouse around so that I can see inside, "I like figuring out what fits where, and how it will affect the dolls that live in the house."

"Do you have names for the dolls?"

She frowns, "No. I never thought they needed names."

## EVERYONE NEEDS A NAME

Sarah laughs.

"What?"

"You are talking to yourself again."

"Oh man," I sigh, the windowpane shaking, "it must be bad if I can't even notice the difference."

Sarah shrugs, "That's what this is all for."

## WHAT IS IT FOR?

"You realize you're asking a child, right?"

I pretend to laugh, "Well, age is relative in my opinion."

"Good answer."

"Thanks."

## WHAT HAPPENS NOW?

Weren't we talking?

I was asking a question, I think.

"You're a wreck, you know that?"

I lie back in the bed, "I know…"

Sarah hands me a doll, "Let's play a game."

## WHAT KIND OF GAME?

"Here, take this doll."
"It's a little girl…"
She makes a face, "So?"

## OKAY, OKAY

Sarah assumes the role of the father, the dad, that doll that had represented me during my theoretical fight.
"We talk like this."
"Like this?" I do my best to mimic the high-pitched voice of a young girl while Sarah does her best to mimic the low guttural voice of an adult male.
She smiles, "Yeah!"
As the dad figure, she asks me, "What round is it?"
"Round ten."
"It's almost over."
I nod, "Yeah it is."
Makes a face.
Whoops, I broke character. In the guise of the doll, I repeat myself, "Yeah it is."
"How does it feel to have ended your career?"
I think about this, "I don't really know what to feel."

## NO ONE IS SUPPOSED TO KNOW
## WHAT HAPPENS NEXT

"That's okay," Sarah replies.

## ALL YOU CAN DO IS PLAN FOR TOMORROW

"You already understand," Sarah laughs, "you just need to admit to yourself that it's time."
"Time for what?"
She moves the doll's arm, a mock-scolding gesture, "You can't keep playing dumb. It's a new era for you. You can be whatever you want to be. You can change whatever you want to change.

If you're lucky, you won't see yourself in the mirror. You'll get to watch from the outside looking in. You get to settle down and appreciate all that you've done."

## SHE'S RIGHT

"I know I'm right," Sarah grins.

In the guise of the doll, I ask Sarah, "Who is your favorite boxer?"

"Willem Floures of course!"

"But what was your best fight, in your opinion?"

"I like this one."

"Which one?"

"The one that's just about to end."

The house is silent, little more than a low rumble from the basement.

## THE PERFECT FIGHT

In that low voice, she tells me, "I don't know if anything can be perfect, but it's been a really great fight."

## I WILL BE REMEMBERED FOR IT

"You will be remembered in general, Willem."

I smile and it's a genuine smile.

I look around the room, to the mirror where I can see my reflection and it's the reflection of Willem at the end of his career.

I whisper to myself.

## IT'S OKAY

Clearly the game is over but Sarah keeps speaking in that voice. "It makes me sound older," she grins.

I laugh, and it's a real laugh, no underlying accusation, no other harm outside of the expression laughter typically brings: humor, hilarity, something said or done that registers pleasant, merry response.

I tell her, "Your dad is going to be busy training 'James.'"
She moves the dollhouse aside.
Sits down on the floor and looks up at me, "I'm going to be busy too. I have to take care of you."

## TAKE CARE OF ME

"You are a wreck, but so was 'James' when Dad retired him."
Everything clicks into place.
I look in the mirror, at my reflection as it begins to fade, but only a little, enough to notice that my stake in the spotlight has completely ended.
And you know what?

## I'M OKAY WITH IT

I exhale, "I guess you are right. I could get used to this."
Sarah asks me, "What do you plan on getting used to?"
I listen to the silence.
I tell her, "I'm going to face the laughter."
She grins.
"I want to change. I want to be something else. Like you said, I get to be the fighter after the fighting. I get to figure out what that means, and I'm okay with that. I choose to embrace challenge. I'll haunt somewhere else."
Sarah breaks character, saying in her own voice, "Yay!"
Yeah. Let the world go on without me. I will be here. I will haunt the areas that heal me, and I will soon be healed. I have time before I turn into someone else. I have time to decide who I'll become.
Sarah grins, "You can only be yourself." She turns on the TV I didn't notice until now and sits on the bed as we watch the final round of the fight.
A moment later we hear the sounds of the house settling.
Getting used to this.
First thing I have to do is break some bad habits. That means this is where I leave you. I can't keep talking to myself. If I keep it up, you might get the idea that none of this really happened

and that's the *last* thing I need. I've played the insanity card and it got me a few wins but one too many punches to the ego. So, yeah, this is where I leave you.

## IT'S ME, WILLEM

It's been real.

# ABOUT THE AUTHOR

Michael J Seidlinger has been in the ring long enough to experience the sting of a perfectly timed power punch. He'd like to think that every novel represents a fight its author has both fought and won. His other fights include *My Pet Serial Killer* and *The Sky Conducting*. He owns and operates Civil Coping Mechanisms, an indie press specializing in innovative fiction and poetry. Find him on Facebook, Twitter (@mjseidlinger), and at michaeljseidlinger.com.